BETWEEN TWO HOMES

Michael Williamson

ONION RIVER PRESS

Burlington, Vermont

Onion River Press

24 Maple Street, Suite 214

Burlington, VT 05401

www.onionriverpress.com

ISBN Paperback: 978-1-957184-45-6

ISBN eBook: 978-1-957184-46-3

Library of Congress Control Number: 2023921276

For my mother, who did not get to see me recover.

<u>Part One</u>

I

In Houston's midtown an odd conglomeration of buildings sat huddled together in a city block across from the light-rail line. Outside the homeless shuffled about, intermixed with the buildings' residents, some hardly distinguishable from one another. These buildings were all operated by the same group of people. They were edificial vestiges of the city's old medical center, with the main, two-story, white, wooden, west-facing, office building (though it only contained a single office) marked *938 Main Street* serving as the complex's headquarters. This office building also served as the dining hall and convalescence ward. The one behind it (also wooden, two-story, and white but east-facing) marked *1083 Fannin* which stood separated by a gravel courtyard, and functioned as the complex's primary living quarters. There were also three two-story, wooden houses on the Fannin side, a gray, a red, and a yellow across the street. Between the primary living quarters and the gray house ran a slim strip of green natural beauty unlike anything else within the immediate area. The only building in this block that the proprietors did not own was a small, abandoned north facing strip center on Alabama of which the only former business still labeled read *Saigon Tailor*. Adjacent to the office stood a third similar white building that served as a place of congregation to both the residents and the community at large. Above this meeting-hall about a dozen of the complex's residents lived cramped in a dimly lit attic space which had in recent years been converted into a makeshift bedroom.

On the sides of some of these old and weathered buildings were sets of two wide doors that stood four or five feet off the ground in the skinny alleyways; so that if one were to open them from the inside and step out without looking, they would fall several feet to the gravel alleyway below. As part of the old medical center, some of them used to be morgues and small clinics, and these doors were where stretchers raised up so that bodies could be brought in and out. However, just because these buildings no longer belonged to the medical center does not mean that these macabre side doors would not have been useful at times. While they were in fact decommissioned, occasionally from within one of these buildings a body accumulated, though this conglomeration had no longer been part of the medical center for quite some time. For over fifty years they had served their current purpose. They had seen an abundance of tragedy, and if their walls could talk, they would tell stories you would not believe.

A truck pulled slowly into the pothole-filled, gravel lot on the block's south side, kicking up clouds of ancient white-gray dust along with it. The two front doors swung open and the two men who got out opened the backseat's doors to an unconscious young man who lay buckled in but slumped over.

"Hey, get up we're here," one said.

The unwitting passenger, who lay uncomfortably in a state beyond stupefaction, made no response.

"We'll come back for him," said the other.

They cracked the windows, closed the doors, and circled round the side of the office building going up its steps and through the front door. In the entryway a middle-aged black man sat dignified behind a wooden desk. His name was Duke.

"Can I help y'all?" he said to the two middle-aged white men who stood looking around before him.

"Yes, I hope so," said Alex who was the shorter of the two and had driven. "I gotta real wet one out in the car," he continued.

"Why don't you bring him in," said Duke.

"He's in real bad shape," said the taller man with slicked back black hair named Liam.

"Well, he gotta be in here for me to do an intake. I can't admit nobody from the parking lot."

"Okay give us a few," said Alex.

They headed back out to the lot. The boy in the backseat still lay incapacitated. They tried to rouse him.

"Get up, you gotta come on inside with us," said Liam.

The boy lifted his head drooling and mumbled incoherently.

"I think we might need to carry him, else he'd lay there all day like a fuckin dog," said Alex.

"Carry him? My back's not good enough for this shit. God, I don't miss living like that."

"Me either. He's gonna feel like a miserable sack of shit when he wakes up," said Alex.

"Good, I hope he remembers that misery. As long as he uses it as the touchstone for progress and not as an instrument for self-pity," said Liam.

"We'll see, I sure hope so, but he can't go on living like this much longer."

"No, it's sad. The candle that glows twice as bright burns half as long," added Liam.

"Candle?" said Alex looking askance. "This motherfucker's been a stick of dynamite ever since I met him."

Liam was quiet a minute.

"Was that the first time you'd met his mother?" he asked.

"No, we've talked briefly a few times."

"Boy, she was madder than hell."

"Rightfully so, I would be," Alex asserted. "Steal my mother's shit and give it to the dopeman. I'd be pissed too."

"She's a good mother and a good woman. For she so loved

him that she would not abet his self-destruction, should he perish, he should do it elsewhere, outside the home, and so she cast away her only begotten son. But if he can come to believe, he should have life and everlasting joy and thus return home."

"Pshhh," said Alex, questioning his friend's biblical grandiosity.

"I'm just sayin," said Liam.

"Anyway," began Alex unswayed. "I'll crawl up in here and grab his legs. You pull him out by his arms, and we'll lug him inside."

Liam pulled his arms while Alex climbed through the back of the truck holding his ankles. They got him.

"Better close the door in this part of town," said Alex.

"Okay I'll have to set him down," replied Liam.

"It don't matter," said Alex. "He can't feel a fuckin thing right now anyway with all that dope in him."

They laid him in the dusty gravel. Liam closed the door. They carried the virtually lifeless body along about ten yards or so.

Alex said, "hold up, I better lock it."

They drooped him face up on the gravel once again. Alex clicked the lock button on his keys twice.

"Alright let's go," he said.

As they carried the body along, the building's residents and various onlookers stood confused. Not by his level of intoxication, they all understood that. But by his age and the look on his face. Though drunken and inscrutable, something on it looked innocent. To the onlookers it seemed an unusual scene. Two men, presumably by the way they dressed, were not from the area and carried between them what appeared to be a dead teenage boy. The boy did not have a shirt on, his pale body splattered with dried mud, wearing torn, long, jean shorts, his face wore a sickly pallor, and he reeked of booze.

"We don't get many in that state anymore," an older man said.

"That's a real one," someone else remarked

The group of five or six men out front chuckled. A train approaching from the south blew its horn in the distance. Only a few blocks over, the sound of the train began to muffle the men's conversation. It again blew its horn.

"Here lemme get the door for y'all," one of the men said.

As he held the door back, the nearing train droned out any other sound. They lumbered with the body up a few steps and into the entryway. Before the door shut behind them, the train passed, blowing its horn one final time. The door shut and the train itself became muffled, but the building shook ever so lightly for just a second.

"Put him over here," said Duke as he drew up a chair next to the desk.

They slouched the body down in the chair. His neck rolled back, and his head hit the wall. Unfazed, he sat motionless.

"I should have asked y'all this before y'all brought him up in here," said Duke. "But does he even want to get sober?"

II

They were all quiet for a minute. Matthew's eyes momentarily fluttered open and then he was gone again. Alex and Liam stood with their backs facing the front window. The evening sun came through the window and from Duke's seat behind the desk their figures stood in silhouette. He reached in the desk and pulled out a clipboard with a small stack of forms on it. Duke heaved a sigh and leaned back in his office chair, it creaked, echoing his frustration.

"So, what's your name?" he said.

Matthew was slowly leaning forward in his chair. With his eyes still closed he ineffectually murmured something while continually hunching his body forward. He almost lost his balance but just before he did his body instinctively snapped back up.

"Signs of life," said Alex.

"Let me get him a cup of coffee," said Duke.

He rose, squeezed between the two men, and turned into an office tucked off on one side of the entryway. Liam looked at Alex.

"This should be fun," he said.

Alex glanced into a rectangular room across the hall from the office. It was unoccupied and contained three beds made up.

From the office a raspy unknown voice was heard.

"Don't just be handin my coffee out now," it said.

"It's for the new guy," Duke told him.

"Especially to no junkie. Whoever it is probably ain't gonna make it anyway," he laughed. "I shouldn't have said that. Well go on, give it to him."

Duke came out and sat on the desk next to Matthew a small Styrofoam cup of coffee.

"Let's try this again. What's your name?"

"It's Matthew," said Alex.

"That's great," said Duke. "But I need him to be able to tell me that."

He took off his hat and placed it on the desk. Alex and Liam scrutinized him. He was about their age, fiftyish. Neither very dark nor light complected, almost ruddy. He had a straight hairline and a goatee with a few grays in it.

"Matthew, what's your last name?"

He mumbled again.

"What was that? Williams?"

Matthew slunk his back against the wall, moved his lips but no sound came out.

"He said Wilkinson."

Duke's chair creaked as he turned to look at Alex, agitated.

"Matthew, what's your date of birth?"

Sitting, looking devoid of life, he made no response.

"Does he have ID?" Duke asked the men.

"Yes, his wallet's in his back pocket. His mother gave it to me for him before we left," said Alex.

"And are you his father?"

"No, no, I'm his sponsor"

"Been working with him long?"

"A couple months. He's still writing inventory. I got it in the truck with the rest of his belongings. This isn't his first slip and now his mom don't want him around."

"What he do?"

"Stole a bunch of her shit and sold it."

"For what, what's he on?"

"I'm not entirely sure. Oxycontin and Xanax, I think."

"Sure smells like a brewery," Duke observed.

"Yeah, that too. You know how we are," said Alex.

The men laughed. Duke's face betrayed a slight smile.

"Y'all doin that intake or not? It's getting late for admissions," said the raspy voice.

A tall black man with a bald head and glasses, wearing a white tank top and cargo shorts emerged from the office. He was probably a little over sixty.

"I'm Hugh, I'm one of the managers," he rasped, extending his hand first to Liam and then to Alex. He looked passed Duke to Matthew slouched back in the chair, head back, eyes closed, mouth open.

"Man, that boy tore up," he said.

The other three nodded in unison.

"We were just about to get his ID out his pocket so I could fill in what I could on the admissions forms and lay him down in the sick-room. When he wakes up, whoever's on duty can get the rest," said Duke.

"Yeah, better do that. If I know one thing, it's that that boy ain't answerin no questions anytime soon," said Hugh good humoredly.

"Why don't I try to lift him by the armpits, and you grab his wallet out his back pocket," said Liam to Alex.

While they did so, Hugh stood perplexed, examining the boy's appearance.

"How'd he get like that?" he said.

"How'd he get so fucked up?" asked Liam.

"No dammit. I know how he got like that. Boy took some shit. Shit he been drinkin too. I can smell his ass from here, all liquored up. What I meant was, how'd he come to be sittin in here with no shirt, torn pant leg, and mud all on him?" said Hugh gesticulating.

"I don't know the whole story," Alex started. "But he stole some of his mother's stuff, sold it, and got high and all that. Anyway, his mother comes home, sees what he did and chases him out the house. Now, I been workin with him a few months, and he never could put thirty days together. Anyways, back to what I was sayin. I'm on my way to our home-group and I'm pullin up to the meeting hall, I turn into the parking lot from off this little two-lane highway, and I see something in the ditch. I look over and it's my sponsee laying face down by the ditch. With no shirt, no sense, no nothin."

The men all chuckled. Hugh shook his head in disbelief.

"And then what?" he said.

"Well I got Liam. We loaded him up in the truck and took him back to his home. His mother wouldn't have him inside the house, had he been able to move. So, she gave me a backpack with some clothes in it and I told her that I knew of a home we could take him. And so here we are," finished Alex.

"Damn shame, a boy that young," Hugh commented.

"Yeah, but if he gets it now, he can save himself a lot of heartache down the road," said Liam.

"Ain't that the truth," said Hugh.

Meanwhile Duke had finished jotting what little info he could from the driver's license. Name: Matthew Wilkinson, age eighteen, with a Houston address.

"I got all I could," he said.

"Well let's get him in the room to detox," said Hugh.

Alex and Liam carried him into the room across from the office and laid him on a bed on top of the sheets. Alex set a scrap of paper with his name and number on it on a nightstand.

"How much is it for a month?" Alex asked Hugh.

"Three hundred and thirteen dollars," said Duke. "For the first month that is. And today bein the sixteenth, means April sixteenth it goes up to five hundred flat from then on."

"Do y'all take credit card?" Alex asked Duke.

"Nope," Hugh quickly said.

"Well, can I bring it by when I come to see him?"

"When will you be back down?"

"Within a week to do some work," said Alex.

"That's fine but if we don't have it in a week, he's out on the street. This ain't no damn flop house," rasped Hugh.

"That's fine, I'll be here. Hey, how long do y'all usually keep them in detox?"

"Oh, it depends. Typically, three to five days. But it's not medical. We don't give em nothin. If there's a stroke or seizure, we just call an ambulance." replied Hugh.

"Well, he's your problem now," said Alex.

"We'll take good care of him. Thanks for bringin him in. The boy needs some help and this the place to set him right."

"Of course," said Alex. "Oh, his stuff."

"I'll get it," said Liam.

He ran out to Alex's truck with the keys and returned with a backpack.

"We'll have to search that, but thanks again," said Hugh.

"No problem."

The two men walked out the front door and into the city street. Instantly, they became coated in the setting sun.

III

It started with a jolt, and the machinery began to move quicker than he had anticipated. As his car moved both out and up, he looked down on empty fairgrounds with carnival lights flashing through the night. The air was cool, and he was alone. "This isn't so bad," he thought. His car rotated steadily towards the top. He exhaled lightly and could see his breath. The car began its descent and the ground did not look so far away as the wheel neared its first full rotation. "I could get used to this," he thought as the car glided smoothly past the turnstile at the rides' entrance. But on the second rotation a shock was felt, and the car slowly began to accelerate. Tranquility disturbed, the mild turning of the wheel was soon brisk and became more rapid. As the car rocked, he held onto the center pole as if it were his mother. He desperately wanted to peer over the side but did not for fear of disrupting the car's already shattered equilibrium. As the car swayed, he felt that he alone was dangling and that nothing stood between him and the ground below. He screamed and stood upright. As he clenched tremblingly to the pole, he could see hundreds of people down below pleading for him to come down. The fast motion made him dizzy and his grip loosened as his palms began to moisten as he started to sweat all over. He thought he might soil himself or lose consciousness as the car crested for a now unknown time. "How long have I been spinning? How long have I been going round and round?" He thought he might jump but at the zenith he lost his balance and fell over the side.

He woke up in a dark room, but light came in through an open doorway. He had pissed himself. He wondered, 'If I'm not in jail or the hospital, where am I? I'm not home. These are sheets and not just a mattress with a comforter, but I've never seen any of this before.' His head ached and spun. He felt he was going to be sick, but his perspiring body clung to the rough sheets. Leaning over the side of the bed to see a waste basket without a liner, he spewed white foam that sloshed into the empty can.

"You alright in there?" he heard from the bright hallway.

He said nothing.

Drenched in sweat, he sat up shivering and placed his feet on the cold floor. He reached to the empty bed across from him and took a wool blanket folded at its foot. Wrapping himself in it, he laid back on his scratchy, sweat and piss dampened sheets and tried without avail to get comfortable. The dark room dimmed further as a shadowy figure stood eclipsed in the lighted doorway.

"Can I get you anything? Water? Something to eat? Aspirin?"

Still not sure where he was, he made no response and rolled over to face the wall.

"Ok, well if you need anything, I'll be right out here."

He knew the figure had retreated because minor light had returned to the wall. 'I don't know how I got here but something's not right,' he thought as fear enveloped him. An unshakable feeling of having committed some atrocity, something unforgivable, consumed him. 'What have I done? What if I killed someone? No, if I had killed someone I'd be in jail or the hospital. But where am I? Where is mom? Is she ok?' Then the worst thought of all popped into his mind. 'What if I've done something to hurt her?' He teared up at the thought.

Shivering in his blanket, he turned over horrific possibilities.
And his yellowed eyes lay fixed on the blank wall before him.

IV

As always, the room was dim. He laid listening to an assortment of ruckus going on outside the door, voices hollered, plastic slammed, and metal clanged. He laid in piss and sweat, but that didn't bother him. He looked at shadows pass on the wall a few feet from his face. One moment he lay motionless, cold, nauseous, starved with dry mouth, and muddled thoughts, yet shaking, overheated, satiated, and focused the next. He felt awful but sat up when he detected the smell of warm food. Unknown faces, some smiling, and some menacing peered in at the doorway as if he were a captured alien on display. Their unclear features due to the light behind them frightened him.

"He up in there?" said an authoritative voice.

"Yeah, he up," one of the figures said.

"You five, go on in there. Wait! I said them five. You be patient and wait your turn. It'll come soon enough," and a figure not small, but disproportionate to the booming voice just heard stepped into the doorway.

"Hey Matthew, you want some dinner?" it said tenderly.

"No, but could you come here?"

"Yeah, what's up?"

"Is there anything I could change in to?"

"Why? Oh, I see. Yeah, you got a bag right here," and he pulled the backpack out from underneath the bed. Matthew glanced not at the unknown faces that peered into the room but at the room's doorless door frame.

"Is there any place I could change?" he asked.

"Yeah, there's a bathroom to the right out there past the desk."

As Matthew squeezed shirtless past the homeless men and women standing in line to eat and turned to push the bathroom door open, he stopped with his hand on the door, and glanced over his left shoulder into the bustling dining hall. Fear overwhelmed him. He felt as though his heart had momentarily stopped. His mind blotted out the commotion, and he couldn't hear a thing. Some fifty odd people ate raucously. Some were in conversation gesticulating while listeners laughed. Others sat at their tables with nobody talking, morosely pushing their food around, and staring down at their trays. A line of people wrapped around the room's perimeter waiting to be served. He forgot what he was doing, and that he was shirtless with his pants soaked through like a child's. He could no longer smell the food, nothing was audible, even the scene itself was beginning to fade away; the only sense he had was his heart thumping. Sweat trickled down his temple, he shivered, and with his hand already on the door, pushed his way into the bathroom.

Like the entire facility, the bathroom was lit with yellow light, so the old and faded white paint on the walls and ceiling were cast in a dull yellow as well. Stepping into the stall and locking it, he opened his bag, and looked at the two clean pairs of shorts, socks, boxers, and shirts he had a piece. He hoped that because he only had two of each that he might not be staying long. "Maybe I'm just here to dry out," he thought. Getting naked to change his clothes, he stood holding his damp boxers and pants, and not knowing what to do with them, put them back into the backpack first, thinking it better to put the one remaining pair of clean clothes on top of the dirty clothes instead of the urine-soaked clothes on top of the clean.

He stood naked, examining his body. He had grown chubby in the almost year he had been out of high school from an indolent lifestyle, eating alprazolam, drinking large amounts daily, getting stoned and passing out on the floor of his bedroom. But his weight wasn't what his thoughts were engulfed in. He stared at his body. He inspected the tattoo of his mother's name across his right arm. He only had three tattoos, but that had been his first. He got it at sixteen late one school night. Attempting to hide it from his mother he wore a shirt around the house nonstop for a week or so until he forgot and came out of his room shirtless. His mother seeing it started to cry, not tears of anger or sadness, but that she knew how much he loved her. She had already known, but that he would mark his body with her name, made her weep, and they hugged intimately telling each other that they would always be there for one another. He stared at the rosary he had tattooed around his neck and hanging down his chest. He got it on his eighteenth birthday to remind him that no matter what he was going through that God was with him. His mother told him not to get it. Though not religious, her mother, his grandmother, was Catholic, and so his mother saw it as sacrilegious. She was so mad when he stumbled in the door that night drunk and shirtless, she started swinging her wooden softball bat from high school at him, hitting him once in the leg, and chasing him out into the front yard with it. His family was not church-going but after everything he and his mother had endured, he thought that there must be a God, or why else were they destined to suffer so much.

Afterwards he studied his mysterious cuts and bruises, wondering as to how he got them. He thought maybe he had jumped a barbed wire fence, but his cuts weren't as severe as the time he had. They were minor scratches. Waking up with random injuries was not an oddity, and he rubbed the thick pink scar that zigzagged up his mid forearm to the knuckle of his left index finger. He was taken back to the night it happened. He was trying to break into a store and cut his hand on a window, hitting an artery and almost bleeding to death. He had run home accelerating his heart rate so that blood shot out his hand ten to fifteen feet with each beat. The memory of the sound it made caused him to shudder. It sounded like when a sprinkler system begins to kick on, *ch ch ch ch*. Then his hand shook so convulsively that he could not get his key in the door, and his hand shot blood all over the left side of his front porch. Inside he went to the kitchen and tried to wash his hand. All he remembered from that was sitting on his kitchen floor with a bath towel trying to clean up the pool of blood while he bled out faster than he could mop it up, and so just ended up pushing a rapidly growing pile around in circles on the white tile floor. He remembered that he had gotten in the shower for some reason, and then just made a shoddy tourniquet with a towel, took some oxycontin, and went to bed. He shook at the memory. He had never told his mom the truth. What he had told her was that walking home drunk on the railroad tracks he had slipped on rocks and cut his wrist open on a broken beer bottle, and that that was how he got the two thick parallel gashes in his wrist and hand. She didn't believe it. She thought that he had been stabbed in a drug deal gone awry. His sister also thought he had been stabbed, but by his mother. When his mother took him to the emergency room to get stitched up his sister had stopped by the house, a somewhat unusual occurrence, to find the entire house splattered in blood. The front porch had been painted red, the white kitchen was a coagulated disaster, the bathtub was a horror scene, and his mattress completely sopped through. But not seeing anyone, she thought that her mother and brother must have engaged in some horrible knife fight, and the survivor fled with the other's body. Nor did the surgeon that reconnected his severed tendons believe his trip and fall story, but he was obstinate in his denial.

He found the dried mud on various parts of his body, even less unusual, having woken up many times caked with the mud from the woods across the street from his house where he often went to drink and smoke, usually with friends but often alone, if he started to get too rowdy for his mother to tolerate.

Staring at his shriveled penis he began to feel emasculated. Not particularly by the look of it as much as the thoughts it aroused regarding his circumstance. He didn't know where he was or how long he had been there or if he had done anything to his mother, and he wondered if she was alright. And so, it hung at half-mast. His eyes watered and he sniffled, and desperately wanted to get drunk and high.

The door creaked open and the noise from the kitchen outside invaded his reminiscence and brought him back to where he was. There was a knock on the stall door.

"Just a minute," he said.

He hurriedly got dressed, zipped up his backpack, and slung it over his shoulder. He opened the stall door and saw a homeless man waiting. The man's white shirt was a dull yellow from both the room's light and being soaked through with sweat and dried many times over. The man quickly walked past him, closed the door behind him, and a violent emptying of bowels was immediately heard. He walked up to the old sink, placed his hands on its sides, and stared at his face in the mirror. He wondered as to what had become of his life. Five or six years ago getting fucked up had been fun. What had happened?

His mind projected his eight-year-old self in the mirror. He wanted to cry at the thought of the boy's innocence, and the naivete that couldn't fathom the pain he would experience in the next ten years. The reflection of his child self morphed into an adolescent version. Still blameless, he speculated that this pubescent self is where he consciously chose to go down a dark path. He wanted to tell this younger self that it was not too late to change. But that was when it was fun, and he would not have heeded his own advice at that age. This image shifted into his poor, sweet mother, who had been through so much between his addiction, his abusively alcoholic but now divorced father, and the heartache of unreciprocated love from his younger sister. His mother was a saint and he wanted to plead with her, to tell her how sorry he was that his addiction had taken precedence in the last four or five years, that he would never leave her side and always protect her from his vindictive father and similarly misguided sister. But the image of his loving mother suddenly became that of his father. It was tall, with tanned skin and jet-black hair but all he saw was a grotesque figure and shook. Feelings of hatred swelled in his heart and he wanted to smash the mirror, but he smelt the man shitting just a few feet away and before he knew it was transported back to the here and now. He stood eyeing the current version of himself in disbelief, freckle faced, green eyed, brown haired, and causer of chaos. 'What have you done?' he thought. He wanted to return to the little boy who had first appeared in the mirror and run to bury his face on the soft skin of his mother's arm but knew that was impossible. He splashed water on his face. Then drying it on his shirt, he gave the current degenerated version of himself with matted, greasy hair and sunken eyes one last look in the mirror. He did not like what he saw and stepped from the shit stenched dingy bathroom back into the musty and clamorous hallway.

V

Matthew stood in the hall and looked at the back of the man sitting at the desk. As it was dinner time, the setting sun shone through the western facing front door both obscuring the features of the destitute who stood in line to eat and intensifying the lackluster hue of the walls.

"One, two, three, four, five, stop," said the deskman.

As he spun his chair around to watch the five people who he let pass to make sure that they went into the dining hall and did not stealthily dip into the bathroom, which was a recurring problem, he saw Matthew standing there cluelessly.

"Want some dinner?" he asked.

"No, I'm not hungry."

"You need to eat something. You been in there sleeping two days now. Probably all dehydrated. Let me get you a tray and some water. Just sit down there and watch them a second."

He was not sure what exactly he was supposed to be watching, but he sat in the chair on the other side of the hall from the desk, just a few feet from it. Without the glow of the evening sky blocking out their images, he scrutinized the homeless men and women standing there. He felt uncomfortable because they all eyed him back. He thought they looked raggedy, but also thought that he was in no position to be judging appearances.

He also thought they smelled bad but recalled that just moments before he was wearing clothes soaked through with piss. Though he were young and white, and they were for the most part older and black, there wasn't any noticeable difference between him and them. He was just as unkempt and rugged appearing and wouldn't have been spotted as an outlier among them.

"Can I use this phone right here? I gotta make a call, it'll only take a second," said the first in line.

"I don't know. Ask that guy when he comes back," said Matthew.

"Why him? You don't work here?"

"No, I don't," Matthew chuckled.

"What's funny?"

"Why'd you think I worked here?"

"Cuz you white."

Matthew's face straightened up and he became serious.

"Look man, I don't even know what this place is called. Let alone work here."

The man returned with a tray and set it on the desk. He looked at the first man in line and then at Matthew.

"Everything alright?" he asked.

"Yeah, he just wanted to know if he could use the phone."

"No can do, sorry," said the deskman.

"Come on, it'll only take a second," implored the man.

"No, it's our policy, sorry," he maintained.

"Well, can we at least eat now then?"

"How many of y'all are there left? One, two…eight. I'm really only supposed to let five in at a time but go ahead.

"Thanks, bossman."

They walked between the two and into the kitchen area. The man sitting across from Matthew was about forty and balding. The few long streaks of blond hair that he had combed back shone like gold in the sun. He motioned at the tray and cup of water on the desk, and Matthew pulled up his chair.

"I got your file here," he said. "While you're eating, I'm

gonna ask you the rest of the questions that Duke wasn't able to get."

"I don't remember answering any questions."

He turned to look Matthew square in the face with his beautiful but penetrating bright blue eyes.

"Yeah, he said you were pretty messed up. All I see that Duke put down really was your name, birthdate, and address. That reminds me," he said while digging through a desk drawer. "This is yours," and he slapped a wallet on the desk. Matthew looked inside, nothing but his ID.

"What's your name?" asked Matthew.

"I'm Dan, they call me Super Dan."

"What's the name of this place?"

"This is The Men's Home. It's the oldest halfway house in Houston. It's really a collection of halfway houses. We own all the buildings on this block except one and then we got a house across Fannin too. People live here, pay rent, you gotta work, attend meetings and all that. Pretty much just pay rent and don't act a fool. We got a meeting hall right next door with a coffee-bar. After you're off detox, you'll go to 1083, the big white house behind this building, where you have to stay at least thirty days before they move you to a less structured house, if and when there's an opening. Any other questions?"

"How much is rent? I just checked, and I don't have no money."

"Your first month was taken care of," said Dan.

"By who? My mom?"

"No, umm," and Dan glanced at the file. "It says here somebody named Alex hasn't yet but will pay."

"Oh, okay then." Matthew's face unconsciously crooked in thought.

"You know him, I'm assuming?"

"Yeah, that's my sponsor. I wondered how I got here. And I don't know why he'd do that. I haven't exactly been the best sponsee. I wonder if my mom knows where I'm at."

"Well, first off, people like to help. He sounds like a good sponsor. He cares about you. Secondly, I'm sure your mother is well aware of where you're at. I mean think, who do you think packed that bag of yours?"

"You're right. I just don't understand how I got here."

"You mean this place in your life? Or here specifically?" asked Dan.

"Well both, but right now I mean here specifically. I mean I must have done something pretty bad for my mom to pack a bag and have Alex bring me here."

His voice cracked while he said this, and he forced his eyes from beginning to water. Dan saw this and suggested he eat some food.

"I hope you're hungry. It's a good night to be hungry. Look, fish patties, mac and cheese, baked beans. It don't get much better than that. I even got you a big piece."

Matthew looked at the square fish patty and though he wasn't very hungry, thought it looked appetizing, and forced himself to nibble a bit. But it was dry and when the breadcrumbs hit his already scratchy throat he began to cough. So, he drank some of his water.

"While you're working on that, let me get started on these questions," he began. "So first and most important, do you want to stop using drugs and alcohol?"

"What I want," Matthew collected his thoughts. "is for all the bad shit to stop happening."

"Yeah," Dan chuckled. "Don't we all? No, but seriously yes or no?"

Matthew thought for a moment, looked down at his food to avoid Dan's powerful blue eyes, and mumbled *yes.*

"Okay, good. So, the next question is, when was your last drink or use? I'm guessing that was two days ago," and he scribbled so on a form. "Okay, what did you drink or use?"

"I just drank a bunch of malt liquor."

"C'mon now, what else you have? You been sleeping in there

two days," pushed Dan.

"Well I eat a lot of Xanax, I take oxy and do cocaine too, but really alcohol and Xanax more than anything," he declared.

"There we go," said Dan. "benzos, opiates, and stimulants. Other than the obvious alcohol."

"Okay," he continued. "When did you start drinking and using?"

"I was probably about eleven when I started drinking and smoking weed."

"Regularly?"

"As often as I could."

"What about the harder drugs?"

"What about them?"

"When did you start using those regularly?"

"Well I started getting a Xanax prescription when I was maybe fourteen or fifteen. Cocaine, when I was a little younger than that, maybe thirteen. As far as painkillers, I've only been taking the strong ones for about two years," he speculated.

"What about heroine, crack, or meth?"

"Yes, not unless freebasing counts, and yes."

"IV?"

"No, I just smoked and snorted."

"Well, that's good," Dan said earnestly, but to Matthew it sounded almost sarcastic.

"Any health problems?"

"The doctor told me that I was prediabetic."

"When was this?"

"About a year ago."

"You do anything about it?"

"No, but he said I could reverse it with lifestyle changes."

"Yep, but you didn't..."

"No."

"Well, you're doing something about that now, I guess. How'd he say you get it?"

"Drinking."

"That figures. You're really young though. Either you drank like a fish or you had a predisposition, probably both." Matthew nodded and Dan allowed a moment to pass.

"Any arrests?" he soon continued anticipatorily.

"Yeah, three."

"Were they violent?"

"Why? Will I not be allowed to stay here if they were?"

"No, I just have to document them if they are."

"One time was for assault and public intoxication," he started.

"Bar fight?" said Dan interrupting him.

"No, at a park. Some guys whooped my ass, and I got arrested," and he thought about how he had instigated the fight by pushing someone.

"And? You were going to go on before I interrupted you."

"Yeah, I don't know if this counts as violent, but another time was for not having a license to conceal a gun, and then I supposedly pulled it out in a public place. But I didn't hurt anyone."

His mind then flashed back to that night. He was seventeen and had just ran out of a store with two thirty-packs of beer. After drinking, he argued with a friend with whom he was sojourning until his brother got out of prison and got out of his car on the side of the road. He called his mother for a ride home and as always, she was there for him. His mother did not know about the pistol and he didn't remember why but he had jumped out of her moving car. Later that night the police pulled up on him walking down the side of a busy road and claimed that someone called and said that he had pulled out a gun in front of them. The officer asked if he was armed, he said no, and when the officer went back to his car to radio that the suspect was allegedly unarmed, he tossed the nickel-plated nine-millimeter in the bushes. Officers found it with their flashlights quickly though because it had been so shiny. He was a junior in high school and was surprised when his mother did not bail him out right away. She wanted him to learn his lesson, and so he sat there for three weeks until his mother realized that he might have to retake the eleventh grade if she did not get him out. He then became angry remembering that his father had visited him while he was in there just to tell him what a piece of shit, he thought he was. When his mother finally bonded him out, she wanted to take him to a drug and alcohol treatment center. With his estranged father in the car, they drove to a treatment center, but he lost all composure and started punching his father in the side of the face while driving down the freeway, causing the car to swerve through multiple lanes. Luckily, it was night and the freeway had not been busy. The only way his mother had been able to calm him down was by feeding him enough alprazolam to tranquilize a horse. He shook at the memory and it made his stomach sour. This recollection took place in a matter of seconds.

"What's the story there?" he asked purely out of curiosity.

"I don't want to get into it."

"What about the third time?"

Matthew's mind mechanically took him back to that day. He was seventeen and walked out of a convenience store with a bottle of malt liquor to see a cop car. Two cops got out and one of them said, "You know, I'm tired of you giving me a bad name." He looked and saw the officer's name was Wilkinson. He had told the cop "Motherfucker, I'm not related to you." Then without asking, the officer reached into his jacket pocket and pulled out an ounce and a half of weed, saying "look what we got here." He handcuffed Matthew and placed him in the back of the patrol car without having searched the rest of his person. Matthew sat in the back of the car wondering what to do with the other ounce of weed in his other jacket pocket. Knowing that there would be absolutely no way for him to dispose of it surreptitiously, he knocked with his head on the car window, and told the officers that they "didn't get it all." This too happened in the blink of an eye.

"That was just pot."

Dan could see that Matthew was starting to shut down and assured him that they were almost done. Matthew was lost in thought elsewhere. He ate all of his fish patty, and some macaroni while he finished off Dan's remaining questions in monosyllables. He was having to confront parts of his past. Disturbing parts, that for so long he had obstinately tried to bury away with continued inebriety. However, now he was defenseless. Thoughts, patterns, memories, dreams, feelings, nightmares both real and fabricated brought terror upon him. Dan was just putting the finishing touches on the forms. When those were completed, he looked up to see Matthew panic-stricken, and colorless with his teeth chattering.

"You okay? You look like you've seen a ghost or something."

He had, his past.

"I just feel sick. Physically, and then trying to remember things that I've been trying to drown out."

"Do you want to lie down?"

"Yes, but do you have a cigarette?"

"Yeah, of course."

Matthew slowly followed Dan down the half flight of stairs and into the cool night.

VI

They stepped out into the fresh air of the March night. It was the time of year in Houston where the days were starting to warm up, but the nights were still cool. In another month or two the heat would start to become unbearable leaving the nights steamy. There was a crescent moon out and Matthew hoped that it was waxing. He disregarded the brightness of the city and focused solely on the moon. Dan hadn't noticed it. Voices and soft rock music were heard not far off coming from a strip of relatively new, trendy bars. They stood only fifteen yards or so from the light-rail tracks, and a train horn blew, signaling its approach from the south on its way into downtown. Though in the heart of the city, to Matthew the night seemed still. He stood in the middle of the sidewalk entranced by the lunar body. A cyclist rang his bell in an effort to tell Matthew to make room, but it did not work, and he went around. Still captivated, Dan nudged him on the shoulder to break his focus and held out his open pack of cigarettes with a lighter. Matthew took one and lit it. Dan broke the silence.

"So, you mentioned your mom. Do you have any other family?"

"Yeah, unfortunately," he said softly, still looking up.

"Brothers, sisters, pop?" Dan said trying to make conversation.

"Dad and sister. They're not around much though. They have their own home."

"Ah, separated. My folks were never together," and he hesitated. "Check this, supposedly Frank Sinatra's my father."

"Uh, what do you mean supposedly?"

"Well, my mom was a dancer in Vegas and Sinatra knocked her up one of the times he came through. Look, I have his eyes." Dan fluttered his lashes.

He did have nice eyes but having little to no idea what Frank Sinatra looked like, Matthew disingenuously assented.

"Yeah, you're right. I see it," wondering if Dan could actually be serious but he clearly was.

"You know a lot of people don't appreciate their parents," Dan started. "I've never met my father. I don't think he ever knew I existed. Years ago, I tried contacting him to let him know that he had a son out there that he didn't know about, but I never got anything back. Think about it, he had a wife and children. He didn't need some kid by a Vegas dancer from years ago coming out of the woodwork. It's okay though. He's dead now, and I'm at peace with it."

Matthew felt that this was a speech he had delivered many times before.

"Anyway, what's your dad like?" Dan innocently inquired.

"We don't get along."

"Just difference of opinion, or was he mean?"

"Both."

"Did he used to hit you?"

"Not me so much as my mom." Matthew's voice got weak.

"I'm sorry, that's rough. Nobody should have to go through that."

"I tried to protect her, but I couldn't when I was little. I wasn't strong enough."

"So, it was mainly directed at your mom?" Dan asked, not realizing the chord he had struck.

"Yeah," Matthew sniffled. "He'd only hit me when I'd get in

the way and try to protect her."

"Mmm," Dan grunted not knowing what to say but wanting to show that he was listening.

"What he'd do," began Matthew. "was knock her out or at least knock her down hard enough to give him enough time to run to the phone and call the police and say that she hit him first so that she'd go to jail. Then once the call was made and she knew that she was going to be arrested, she'd fly at him in a fury to at least make it worth it." He paused and remembered her saying "if I'm gonna go to jail for hitting you, I'm going to at least fucking hit you." Then he remembered the police hauling his mom off one of those nights, with a beaten face, having believed the words of his hammered father. As a young boy, he had pleaded with the officers not to do so. He told them that they "were making a mistake, my dad started it, not my mom. He hit her!" Then his memory of that specific night recalled something he had until then entirely forgotten. He remembered after the police were gone his father asking if he and his sister wanted pancakes and stood swaying in his boxers drunk in the kitchen with pancake mix and a griddle. The callousness and oblivion made him shake, how could one be so cruel?

He continued, "When I was little, I'd try to step in between them to protect her but he'd throw me to the side. Then when I was about thirteen, I thought I was a man, and when I'd see him zone in on her to attack, I'd cock back and hit him as hard as I could in the face. But he'd be drunk and couldn't feel a thing. Then he'd beat my ass, not like a child but like a grown ass man. One time, he grabbed me by the neck and lifted me off the ground, choking me. I remember my mom screaming "get your fucking hands off him, let him go!," and hitting him until he dropped me. Then he turned his attention to her, but realizing, in his drunkenness, what he had done to me he ran to his car to take off. My mom and I chased him into the driveway punching him while he tried to get the car into gear until he started it and ran over my foot."

Matthew started breathing heavily and paused again. He wanted to burst into tears but checked himself. No longer looking at the moon, he sat down on the sidewalk. He was seething with anger. It raged inside him. Not at what his father had done to him, but what he had done to his innocent, loving, and defenseless mother. The hatred swelled inside him as it had many times before, but he had not been faced with such animus without drink or drug since probably one of those nights long ago. He felt weak and emasculated at the thought of his inability to adequately defend his mother. He wanted to drink, but he didn't have any money, and wouldn't have a bed to lie in or food to eat if he did. He lifted his eyes from the ground to the south where he saw the front lights of another train coming. The pity, remorse, and savage animosity that swirled in his heart were becoming a dangerous concoction. If he couldn't drink, and he couldn't be with his mother, he ought to just leap on the tracks and put an end to his sorrow. The train blew its horn as his emotional mixture was nearing fatality. Dan watched him but had neither idea as to the severity of his current emotional climate, nor what he was contemplating. However, something divine came over him as the train got close. He thought of the effect that his death would have on his mother. He could not abandon her. The hate and enmity flowing through his being began to subside and were reclaimed once again by misery. The train flew by. He just couldn't do it. No amount of pain could bring him to leave his mother alone, in a hostile and cruel world in which his father was allowed to roam free.

He quietly began to cry. Like his feelings of anger, his sadness quickly intensified, and he wailed on the sidewalk with tears streaming down his face. Dan just stood there for a while and let him get it out, and then offered him another cigarette. As Matthew pacified, Dan softly said, "time heals." Matthew was taken aback, annoyed and insulted by the platitude. He lashed out.

"You think I outta be grateful for my father. Go fuck

yourself," he spewed.

"Hey buddy, that's not what I meant by that. I didn't mean nothing by it."

He thought back to Dan's phrase *time heals*. It made him sick. He could not envision his deep-seated fatherly hatred ever relenting.

"You know," Matthew sniffled as he began. "I'd much rather not have ever met my father, like you, than have to go through what I've dealt with."

"Me too bud," Dan acquiesced.

As the second cigarette burned, Matthew slowly calmed. In general, his rationality and reason needed an entire overhauling, but as he turned over ideas in his head, trying to block out his powerful feelings and think objectively, there was a faint glimpse of the possibility of their restoration. He stood up, and once again looked toward the moon, and under his breath he said, "No matter what it takes, I'm gonna earn her trust back and show her how much I love her."

VII

He woke up grumpy, sweating, and with a headache. He went out to the desk, and asked Duke, a man he had never seen before, what time it was. It was almost lunch. He went to the bathroom, and after gulping down water from the sink, he stopped to look at himself in the mirror. He did not see his true figure so much as he saw what he considered to be the epitome of perdition. He could not think straight, but knew he wanted to get away from his reflection. Walking back to the sick-room Duke said, "I almost forgot to tell you, your sponsor called and said to finish writing your inventory today. And that he'll be here tomorrow to go over it." This bothered Matthew, and he asked if he could use the phone.

"I guess so, but don't be too long. I gotta keep this line open."

Matthew pulled up a chair and dialed his home phone, but no one answered. He didn't care to leave a message.

"What day is today?" he asked.

"Tuesday," responded Duke without looking up from his book.

'Okay, mom's at work,' he thought.

"I'm gonna try one more number," he said.

"Go ahead but make it quick."

And Matthew called his mother's cell. It went straight to

voicemail. Hearing her voice, he realized that he had no idea what he wanted to say.

"Mom, umm, it's Matthew. I just wanted to call to see how you were. Call this number back when you can… I love you," and he hung up.

"No answer?"

"Nope," mumbled Matthew.

He walked back to the sick-room feeling defeated. He sat on his bed for a little bit, not thinking, just staring at the floor. He reached under his bed and pulled his spiral from his backpack. It smelt like piss, and he thought it proper. He flipped it open just a few pages to where he had left off writing. He had already written the people down that he was mad at. That was easy. He also had already finished writing why he was upset with them which he had embellished. The last section that he had completed was identifying the root of just why exactly the actions of others hurt him and remembered that that part hadn't been too difficult either. So, he looked at the section that he had to finish by the next day which was what he had done to other people. The thought of not only summoning those memories to the forefront of his mind, but also to then divulge those actions made his head spin. But he thought it best to get it over with sooner rather than later. 'Okay, here we go,' he thought.

The first name was his father's. 'I've never done anything to him,' he told himself. 'Definitely nothing serious or worth putting down.' So, he moved on to the next name, God. He thought for a minute but couldn't think of anything he had done to God. Like his father, he had been blameless, and so he moved on to the next name. It was Bella, his high school girlfriend. He thought about what he had done to her. 'Well, I got her pregnant, and convinced her to get an abortion.' He really felt terrible about that. At the time he thought maybe a child would be what he needed to straighten his life out, but he was seventeen and she was only sixteen. She was Catholic, and her mom was okay with it in order to keep the fact from her father that his little girl had not only been having sex but had also gotten pregnant. Her mom had only asked him to pay for half of it, and he said "no, I'll pay for the whole thing." Then when the day came, he publicly humiliated her when he showed up to the clinic with four-hundred dollars in quarters, from his childhood piggy bank, tied off in a black trash bag. He and a clerk counted out the coins on a desk while Bella cried with her face in her hands. But he was short twenty-five cents, because one of the quarters was Canadian. So, he ran to his bank to withdraw a quarter. The female teller laughed at him, and asked what he needed it for, and then looked at him disgustedly when he told her an abortion. Afterwards, he brought her flowers. The next day at school she had been depressed so he gave her several alprazolam. Later he heard from people that she fell out of her stool during science lab and was arrested for drug possession. She didn't rat him out but never spoke to him again, and he was hurt and angered by that. "Matthew lunch," rang Duke's voice from the hall, snapping him out of his memory. 'I need to put something down. I did cause her a significant amount of harm and embarrassment.' So, he wrote 'treated her poorly,' and thought it sufficient because it was true.

Walking into the hall perturbed, he asked Duke what was for lunch, and was told soup and sandwiches, and this annoyed him further. Stepping coyly into the dining hall, he got in the back of the line for sandwiches. There weren't many people there yet but avoided looking at other people's eyes for fear of being sucked into conversation. The line moved quickly, and when it was his turn the old black man wearing a name tag that said *Chef Davy* said in a toothless voice, "You been here several days now, and I ain't seen you in here once yet. That means you get two sandwiches. Eat those up and get some strength in you."

"Thank you."

He took his tray over to get a bowl of soup, and then found an empty table. Soon two men in conversation sat their trays opposite each other at his table so that he was sitting next to both. They carried on for a minute about something he neither understood nor cared about. They soon stopped. He didn't like the silence. He knew that he was about to be targeted for small talk. "Sick-room eh," said the middle aged bald white man to his right, Matthew nodded. "We're two of the house managers over at 1083 where you'll be as soon as you get off detox. I'm Robert, and this is also Robert." Conversation with one person was burdensome enough for Matthew, but now he had two sets of eager eyes looking at him.

"How's it going?" he managed to spit out.

"Not too bad," said the equally short but older other Robert with a buzz cut and glasses to his left. "What about you?" he continued.

"I'm good," said Matthew quietly.

The two Roberts looked at each other and laughed.

"What's so funny?"

"It's okay, we know you're not doing good. No one is when they first get here. Hell, I wasn't. You should have seen Robert here," and he pointed to the older one to Matthew's left.

"He's right. I was miserable. But it gets better."

"Well, that's good to know," and Matthew recoiled.

They realized he didn't want to talk. So, they picked their conversation back up from when they had sat down. Their laughter resumed, and Matthew found it contemptible. 'What about any of this is funny,' he thought. A series of bitter thoughts took hold of him. His ears were shut off, but he pretended to pay attention by nodding his head every so often. 'No, really I don't see any humor in this.' He looked around the room. It was old and wooden. It creaked constantly as people shuffled about. Even though it was full of food, it had a mustiness that never left. The dull yellow light was dim. His chair was hard, the table wobbled, his sandwich dry. 'They're fucking with me.' He found both their words cruel and their joke sick. 'Nobody could find any of this enjoyable. If they're alcoholic like I'm alcoholic, they wouldn't be sitting there laughing. They don't know what pain is. They're mocking me.'

He thought about the people at his home-group, and how they laughed. 'They're fake too. That's why Alex wants me to write all the horrible things I've done down. So, he can join in their ridicule. Why would he do that? What if they're all in on this together? They didn't drink like I drank or else they wouldn't be happy. Look at them, with their smug faces. They think I don't know. They think I'm a fool. You don't go through all that I've gone through being dumb. I'll show them.'

'No, wait am I crazy? Or am I just going crazy, but I'm not quite there yet. No, what if I've been crazy? And those were the first thoughts of me coming out of my delusion. No, I'm insane. There's no grand plot against me. But what if there was? What if I never did anything to mom? What if she just got sick of me and wanted me out of the house? She wouldn't do that. What am I thinking? Alex didn't set anything up. How could he? Well, I suppose he could if he wanted to. But why?' He looked back and forth between the two Roberts. 'No, they're really laughing. That's genuine laughter and they're having a good time. How come I never have a good time? Because I'm always either drunk or high. No, that can't be it. I'm not drunk or high now and I'm miserable. God must hate me. But why? Why does he hate me? Does mom hate me? Oh god, What have I done?'

"Hey, why don't you go lay down?" said the older Robert.

"What? Why?" asked Matthew.

"Well," he began. "you look like you're gonna be sick, you're pale, sweating, and you've hardly touched your food. You've been staring off into space mouthing words to yourself this whole time. You're detoxing, probably behind on sleep and could use the rest. And you just don't look too hot. Want me to go on?"

"No, you're right," and Matthew got up from his paranoid dejection and staggered back to the sick-room.

Sitting on his bed he picked his spiral back up. As agonizing as it was to face those feelings of guilt, and the shame that usually followed he thought that he would be better off just getting it over with. He glanced at the list, but it was too much for him. So, he thought of something brilliant. 'I can just make up wrongs,' he thought. 'I can just make up things that I didn't do that are bad, but not as bad as the things I actually did do. Alex will never know. That way he'll be happy, and I can still take all those secrets to the grave. It's perfect.' He prided himself at such ingenuity and breezed his way through the list of names fabricating minor harms and disclosing half-truths. Content with his work, he stretched out on the bed with his hands behind his head and fell into a deep sleep that went through dinner.

VIII

He was at the beach with his mom. It was a sunny day, and he went out for a swim while she laid out on the sand. The waves weren't too rough, so he leisurely swam out, paddling on his back. Floating, he could hear children's voices and playful splashing close by. He could see storm clouds in the distance, but they were a ways off, and not an immediate threat. He felt the small waves rocking him gently in the water and he closed his eyes. Only a moment had passed but all was silent. Flipping up and treading water he was alarmed to see the sky darkening. He had floated much further out but he could still see what he thought was his mother looking around. Thunder cracked. He put his head down, kicked his feet, and thrust his arms towards shore. After a few minutes, he looked up again. The undertow had pulled him even further out. The sky was now completely black. He could still see the shore, but his mother was no longer there. A bolt of lightning shot out from the sky, and he was beginning to grow tired. He kicked his feet vigorously in one last attempt to get to shore but he could see himself being drug out further by the second. He was exhausted. Shore was no longer in sight. His head went under.

Matthew woke up hungry. There was a dim light that came in through the hall. He was drawn to it and went out. Hugh sat quietly at the desk reading under the glow of a faint lamp light. He hadn't noticed Matthew step up.

"Hey, uhh is there any way I could get something to eat?"

Hugh looked up abruptly and wide eyed.

"Dammit, how long you been standin there?"

"Just a minute."

"Oh, well dinner's been done," he rasped.

"Okay, I was just wondering…"

As Matthew turned to walk away, his pitiful face caught Hugh's eyes with a force with which he later could not explain.

"You want some cereal? We got some cereal in there."

"Yeah, I'll take some cereal," said Matthew, relieved at the idea of food.

"Well, come on then," and he slapped his book down open faced on the desk. Matthew followed him into the kitchen. They each returned to the entryway with a bowl and settled themselves comfortably in the yellow light. Each munched without saying a word. Hugh had returned to his place in the book. Matthew scrutinized him in the dull lamp light wondering who this man was. Hugh looked up and studied Matthew.

"Matthew, just how old are you?" and he set his book down.

"I'm eighteen."

"God," Hugh exclaimed. "What it is to be eighteen."

"I'm sorry, what is your name?" inquired Matthew.

"I'm Hugh, I'm one of the managers. Well, assistant manager that is. We'll see for how long though."

"I'm Matthew."

"I know who you are dammit," and he chuckled. "I was here when they drug yo drunk ass up them steps."

Matthew was quiet. Hugh stared off with a look of bewilderment across his face.

"Eighteen," he repeated in dismay.

Matthew remained silent.

"You know," he said, clearing his throat. "I left home at eighteen. Grew up in a small town outside of Mobile. Only been back once, in all these years, when my momma died." He shook his head, while still looking off in the distance. "When I was eight my daddy got picked up for vagrancy on his way home from work. Never saw him again." His eyes moistened. "I always wondered what they did to him." Matthew sat laser focused. He couldn't put it into words, but he was attracted to this man. "That's why I got away when I was your age. I knew I had to after what happened to my dad and all. My mom had had cousins that come out to Houston. So, I thought that's where I'll go. Sister come out a few years after me." A single tear ran down his face, and he coughed both to clear his throat and to compose himself. "This December will be twenty-five years since she passed. Where does the time go? Twenty-five years," he said contemplatively.

They sat in silence for a bit. Hugh had poured his past, his heart, out to this white kid he had never met before, and Matthew soaked up every word. After a minute he spoke.

"How'd she die?"

"Crack cocaine… went into cardiac arrest. I just don't know why it had to be her. I was on the shit too. But you see it's not for me to understand. That's for God. I wouldn't understand why he do what he do even if he told me." There was a brief pause. "Do you believe Matthew?"

"Uh," he fumbled his words. "Yeah, I believe in something."

"Good, that's good. I'm glad to hear that. It don't take a lot of faith. At least not at first. And it don't look like you got much. But that's okay, because it only takes a little bit," and he held his thumb and his index finger close together up to his eye to demonstrate just how little it took. "That of a mustard seed," he continued. Matthew did not get the reference but understood. He was fascinated but not convinced. Another minute or so of quietude passed between the two.

"What he can do is miraculous. It's beautiful, his grace that is. Back when I was on that shit, you woulda thought the pipe was glued to my lips. Hell, that was probably before you was born but you get what I'm sayin." Matthew nodded because he did. "I seen people come in here all throwed off, hopeless to the point where I almost told em you might as well walk right back out that door and twist off some more cuz you ain't getting it. But God is good. God is good. They come here broker than hell. They stop putting that shit in their body. Get them a shower. Start eatin right, sleepin right. Start goin to meetings. Do the work. They get theyselves a job. Become productive members of society. When they get here their families don't want nothin to do with them. Can you blame em? But when they put the work in, God starts to put they life back together."

Matthew felt the ardency with which Hugh spoke. He wanted to believe as he believed, but just was not there yet, and was not sure he would ever be. Matthew genuinely wanted to get better though. He wanted to do it for his mother more than anything. He remembered his words from the night before 'no matter what.' 'I just don't have the same passion that Hugh has though,' he thought. 'Does that mean that I won't ever get it? What is it anyway? Belief? That alcohol and drugs could no longer rule my life? That I get to go home? A happy life? I don't want to be like a religious fanatic though.'

Hugh also sat plunged in thought. 'I like this boy,' he thought. 'There's something about him. He doesn't seem like all the rest. I can see it in his eyes. That boy's been through some pain. He has that look, that of a heavy heart. I hope he doesn't bolt, sticks around, and lets God in. God, I sure hope he gets it. Lord, let this young man seek you, if it be your will to enter into his heart so that he may find you, and most importantly, know you dear God. Please lord, absolve him from his ways so that he may experience your mercy. Please bestow your grace upon him so that he may grow in your infinite love.' Hugh then remembered his sponsor Alex and that other man. 'What was his name?' And about what happened between Matthew and his mother. 'Please lord, I pray that you heal this young man's family. Allow this boy's mother to channel some of your mercy and forgiveness so that their family may come together in your love. In the meantime, I ask you to look after his mother, and guide this young man in all his activities. I pray in your name, heavenly father.' He cleared his throat and said softly but aloud "Amen."

"What?" said Matthew.

"Nothing, just talking to myself." After a moment's delay Hugh said, "It's late, why don't you get some rest." So, Matthew went to bed. But for a while he thought about the state of his soul before falling asleep.

IX

Matthew awoke feeling sick and hungry. It was quiet and the sick-room was full of natural light coming in through the hallway. He rubbed his eyes and tried to remember how long he had now been there. He wasn't sure. It felt like he had been there a week, but he could only recall a few days. Getting out of bed, he put on his last pair of clean clothes. The spiral on his nightstand caught his eye. 'Oh shit, that's today,' he thought. He saw Alex's sticky note on the nightstand and wondered what time he would arrive but did not feel like calling him. Sighing, he walked out into the hall. Duke sat at the desk reading. Seeing Matthew, he looked up.

"Need anything?" he asked.

"Is there anything to eat?"

"You missed breakfast by a few hours but there's cereal in there."

"Okay, I'm gonna get some," Matthew declared.

"Do you know where it all is?"

"Hugh showed me last night."

Duke was pleased that he could continue reading. A minute later, Matthew returned with a bowl, and sat eating across the desk from Duke. Duke just lifted his eyes momentarily before returning to his story. Matthew sat eating and thinking about a cigarette.

"Do you happen to have," started Matthew with a mouthful, "a cigarette I could bum?"

Duke heaved a sigh, put his book down, and reluctantly pulled a cigarette from his pack. He rolled it across the desk to Matthew.

"Thanks," said Matthew munching.

He finished his bowl, walked back to the kitchen to put it in the sink, and then back up front, passed Duke, down the steps, and out the door. Stepping outside hurt his eyes. He had not gotten a lighter, and so went back in the comparatively dark entryway. Picking up Duke's yellow lighter from the desk, he asked if he could use it.

"As long as you bring it right back," Duke said, slightly annoyed.

Returning outside, he found some shade under a tree on the sidewalk. He looked around at the street. It was much different from the other night. The train station was bustling a block away. Construction workers walked around the large lot across the street. They seemed to have just fenced it off to get their project underway. He lit the cigarette and immediately became lightheaded. 'I gotta get me some more of these,' he thought. 'But how?' He had no idea how. Alex was coming later but he didn't smoke. 'Maybe I could ask him for a few bucks.' But he thought about how Alex was going to pay for his entire first month, and he did not want to take advantage of his kindness. He didn't want virtually his only connection to home to think that he was only trying to get stuff out of him.

It then hit him that he might humble himself and ask his father for a little money. 'But I'm not saying sorry to that piece of shit for anything,' he thought. His mind then went back to the last time he saw his father. It had been about six months prior, and at that time it had been about a year and a half since he had last seen him. Matthew and his friend did not have any liquor, and Matthew had come up with a plan. He contrived to knock at his dad's door and feign wanting to catch up with him.

Matthew would chit chat with him until the first opportunity presented itself, and then he would snatch up as many liquor bottles as he could and run off. Matthew had thought it fool proof. So, they drove to his dad's apartment. He went up to the second floor and knocked. A moment later the door swung open. His dad stood confused for a second not recognizing his son with the thirty or so pounds he had gained since he had last seen him. After realizing this rough and raggedy young man was his estranged son, he was confused as to why he was at his doorstep randomly and became embittered.

"What do you want?" he said skeptically.

"I was just in the area and thought you might want to catch up." He remembered how stupid he had thought this sounded when he said that since he only lived about ten minutes away. His father had turned around and left the door open, indicating that he could come in. Though Matthew knew where his father lived, he had never been inside. His father held his hand out over his couch and told him to, "take a seat." Matthew remembered feeling extremely uncomfortable, but he had gone too far to back out now.

"Water?"

"Sure."

"Who was that?" his sister had said emerging from her room.

Matthew's dad looked resentfully over to the couch. His sister hesitated for a moment with her mouth agape. Whether this was from not recognizing him or disbelief he didn't know. She ran over to the couch, bent over, and wrapped her arms around him. He recalled the mixed emotions he experienced then. He loved his sister, but she had chosen their father over his mother, and that hurt his mother, and so she became the enemy. Matthew's father walked up and set a glass of ice water on the coffee table and took a seat. Matthew did not know what to say but he remembered feeling base. Just then a phone rang from another room.

"I'll be right back," his father had said and walked away.

'Here it is. Now's my chance,' he had thought. He spotted a number of cheap wine bottles on top of the fridge. So, he stood up and nonchalantly sauntered into the kitchen.

"What are you looking for?" his sister had asked suspiciously.

"Oh, nothing," he said, trying to keep cool to buy himself time. He had reached up over the fridge and tried to grab the necks of three bottles in each hand, but his strained wrist had still been at less than full strength from surgery months prior. So, he grabbed two in his left, and three in his right, and started for the door.

"Matthew stop! What are you doing?" she shouted.

Matthew could not turn the knob with his hands full, so he set the two bottles in his left hand down for a moment. As he opened the door, his father appeared in the doorway on the other side of the living room with a phone in his hand and said, "I'm going to have to call you back."

He had charged at his son. Matthew picked the two bottles up off the carpet and started to run down the cement flight of steps that went to the parking lot. But he slipped. His feet came out from underneath him and heard the wine bottles shatter at each of his sides as his hands instinctively went down to try and break his fall. He rolled and tumbled down the cement steps. He jumped up, adrenaline pumping, and quickly examined himself. He recalled the white Rockets jersey that he had been wearing became splattered and soaked with red wine. He looked as if he had been shot. His father was almost down the steps, and so he ran the twenty or so yards to his friend's waiting car. As he ran, he heard his sister's voice ring out, "Matthew stop! Please don't go! Come back!" But Matthew had jumped into the car, and they drove off.

'I wonder if he's still mad,' he thought. 'I'd still be. Better not ask him for anything. No, I'll ask. The worst he can do is say no. Plus fuck him.' Matthew flicked his butt in the street and stepped back into the diminished light of the entryway. His eyes had not adjusted, and he stumbled going up the steps. He placed Duke's lighter on the desk and asked to use the phone.

"You know my policy," grumbled Duke.

Matthew picked up the phone and his heart began to beat quickly. He was surprised at this sudden nervousness. In his heart he knew that his mom would eventually forgive him, but he was not sure he and his father would ever be on speaking terms. The idea of him and his father never having a relationship hurt him in a way that could neither be seen nor felt, and therefore expressed. He wanted a fatherly relationship and figure but not with his father, not after what he had done to his mother. In Matthew's mind, what his father had done to his mother forever justified any mistreatment, using or manipulation on his part towards this man. He dialed his number. No one answered, and he hastily thought of what to say on voicemail.

"Dad, it's Matthew… I'm staying at," and he held his hand over the phone. "What's the address?" he asked Duke.

"938 Main Street."

"938 Main Street," he continued. "I don't know how long I'll be here, but I don't have any money and was wondering if I could get a few bucks." Matthew paused, unsure if he should go on. "Anyway, call this number back," and he hung up. He returned to the sick-room and sat on his bed. A moment later Duke knocked on the doorframe.

"Robert the head house manager over at 1083 is going to be over in a minute to take you over there so that you can shower."

"Okay, thanks," Matthew responded thinking of how nice a shower sounded.

"Yeah, no problem. No offense but you need it. You've been sweatin those toxins outta your system for a few days now." And he walked back to the desk. A minute later there was another knock at the door frame. The younger bald-headed Robert was standing there.

"You ready to go get a shower?" he asked.

Matthew followed him out a door in the kitchen that he did not know existed. It opened to a gravel lot. On the other side of the lot was the back of a similar looking two-story building. Looking back Matthew noticed this other building was wider. The gravel lot functioned like a courtyard but had wooden pallets and plastic crates scattered about. A dumpster sat overflowing and rancid with black flies swarming around it. A colony of cats roamed the lot, most laid now in the shade of the few trees located around the lot's edges. Instead of walking in this building's back door, Robert followed a footpath that meandered through a heavily shaded area on the building's right side if coming through the lot. A peace came over Matthew as the city's hustle and bustle along with his ubiquitous anxiety inexplicably dissipated. Robert stopped about midway through and gestured to the narrow alleyway that had long ago been converted into a natural sanctuary.

"This is the Serenity Garden," he said.

Matthew loved it. It was an urban glen, a strip of wooded oasis that offered refuge in the heart of the city.

"Come this way," said Robert.

Matthew did not want to leave but followed Robert around the corner and onto the sidewalk. They headed up a few steps and through a door. Upon entering, Matthew looked to his left to see the older Robert sitting in a decent sized room behind a desk. To his right was a living room with several couches and a tv. Directly in front of the doorway was a very tall wooden staircase. In front of Robert sat a folded bath towel with a bag that contained travel sized toiletries on top of it. Though there were similarities between the main office building and this one, Matthew felt the latter more comforting, even if only slightly. Like the office building, which really only contained one office but also the intake and lobby area, the sick-room, kitchen, and dining hall, this building seemed to be illuminated throughout the day entirely by natural light. Matthew hoped that when the lights came on that they would not be so dull and yellow like the other building.

"Did Hugh mention you'll be moving in here tomorrow?"

asked the Robert from behind the desk.

"No," replied Matthew, overcome with fear.

"Oh yeah," said the younger Robert standing beside Matthew. "Let me show you which bed will be yours."

Matthew followed him up the long staircase. Most of the steps creaked on the way up. At the top, Robert took a right into a large and quite long rectangular room that held eight beds. Through the doorway, Robert stopped at the first bed to the left in one of the corners. "This is yours," he said. "You can put your belongings underneath the bed as well as in the top two drawers of this dresser." Robert stood with his finger on his chin thinking for a moment. "I can't remember his name right now, he's not much newer than you but he gets the bottom two drawers as well as the right half of the dresser top. I can't believe I can't think of his name. Oh well, it doesn't matter right now. You'll meet him." Matthew looked at the long room, symmetrical, with four beds on each side running along the walls. Dust particles shone like glitter as the sunlight hit them while they flittered about.

"How many people live here?" he asked worriedly.

"Forty right now I think," he answered casually. "But there's forty-four beds."

"How many in this whole place?"

"One hundred and twenty, a hundred and twenty-two, somewhere around there."

"Wow, I didn't realize so many people stayed here."

"Yeah, but you gotta remember there's three other houses, and then there's a dozen or so people that live above the coffee-bar."

Matthew still thought it a lot of people. Robert gave him a quick tour upstairs though Matthew wasn't sure why. They were just four other rooms, identical to his, each with eight beds and shiny floating dust particles. Walking back downstairs, Matthew followed Robert, towel and supplies in hand, to the back of the house. There was one other small bedroom. Matthew got a chill that ran down his back. 'All these beds, this giant house, but no one here.' It did not sit right with him and he thought it eerie.

"Where is everyone?" he asked, almost alarmed.

"Oh yeah," and he chuckled. "Maybe I should have led with that. Monday through Friday everyone's gotta be out of the house from nine to three either working or looking for work. Unless of course you work nights." Robert waited a minute to see if Matthew had another question, but he didn't.

"So anyway, around the corner here we have the smoking room. It's the only room in the house that you can smoke in. It's also the only room where people can use electronics."

"What if you don't smoke but you want to use your phone?"

"Well then, you gotta do it in here," Robert affirmed.

Matthew wondered about forty something odd people standing in this 10x15 foot room smoking and making phone calls. But all he said was, "cool."

"And here's the bathroom," began Robert again walking through the smoke room.

"I don't need to give you details on that; I mean it's a bathroom. Just in the morning try to be mindful about shower time. We got forty guys all tryin to get to work so cap it off after about ten minutes. Just between me and you the one on the right stays hot the longest."

Robert gave him a quick pat on the back and walked out. Matthew stood there for a minute. There were four stalls, one with an out-of-order sign on it, three urinals, and three showers. Matthew walked to the one furthest to the right, ran water, and stripped. He stepped in and felt instant relief. The water poured soothingly over his body. He opened the curtain and grabbed the little shampoo and body wash bottles they had given him off the bench. At first the running water had begun to lull his mind, but after lathering his body it had a counter effect. 'I'll be here a month tops, maybe two,' he thought. 'They cram enough people into this house? I hope the guys are cool. I wonder if I'm gonna have to fight anyone. No, this isn't jail. But if they want

it, they can get it. I hope it doesn't come to that. No, it won't.
I can get on just about anywhere. I just need to sit tight, and
mom'll let me come back home. I still need to find out what
I did. Whatever it is, I just need to explain to her that I didn't
mean to, that I'm sorry, and that it won't happen again. I just
hope that she's mad and not sad. Her anger is scary, but I can
deal with it. I can't stand to see her hurt. I'm gonna have to get
a job. Where? Fast food, I guess. That's all the experience I have.
Fuck, I hate working in fast food. I wonder if he'll call me back.
What an asshole. He better not do anything to her while I'm
gone. Not if he knows what's good for him. I'll catch a bus up
there to stick a screwdriver in his stomach. But if he calls back
just play nice. Agree that you've been a selfish prick, don't be
rash or whatever it was Sun Tzu said. And with mom just be
patient. It's not if she'll take me back but when.'

He stepped from the shower, dried, and got dressed. He
combed his hair with his fingers brushing it back while patting
down the parts that stood up with his palm. Not knowing what
to do with his towel he hung it up on a drying rack. He walked
back out to the office area. The two Roberts were in conversation. The older of the two stopped for a minute and said,
"lunch is ready," and then went on talking. Matthew walked out
the front door towards the kitchen. He was hungry.

X

Alex neared the Home where he had dropped Matthew. He counted with his fingers on the wheel. It had been four full days now and he wondered how Matthew was getting on. 'He can't be doing too great,' he thought. His mind drifted from the road before him to his own rehab experience. It had been thirteen years since he was released from state jail with a resolution to never drink again. 'But I also didn't want to do the work,' he remembered. He had only been able to hold out a few days before he succumbed to drink and thereby on the rocks once again. Fear of prison drove him to check himself into a drug and alcohol rehabilitation center. 'But I didn't do the work,' he recalled again. He had left thirty days later cheery faced and steadfast in his newfound life to find himself begging on his knees of the porch of that same rehab a week later. 'That time I was ready. I had had enough,' he thought smiling. "God, that sucked. But it finally got me to do the work," he whispered this last line to himself pulling into the gravel lot. 'I hope it doesn't take him as many times as it took me… '

Matthew sat eating a sandwich both not looking at people nor avoiding their gaze. He heard a knock on the doorframe. Alex stood there grinning.

"How's it going, bud?" he asked.

"Not too bad," Matthew mumbled through his sandwich crammed mouth.

"Feel like dog shit?"

"Yeah, but I've been eating and sleeping, and I took a shower this morning."

"Gratitude, I like it," he chuckled. Hurry up and finish your food. We got work to do."

Matthew got up and threw the rest of his food away, dumping an entire bowl of tomato soup in the trash. He followed Alex into the entryway.

"Mind if we use this room?"

"Not at all. Go right ahead," said Duke.

They stepped into the dusty and pale colored sick-room. The natural light from the hall had just started to creep back over the room's threshold. Alex looked around the sick-room for a moment and took a seat on the bed adjacent to Matthew's unmade one.

"How much longer you gon be in here?" he asked.

"They said tonight would be my last night," responded Matthew gloomily.

"Don't worry," Alex began. "It'll do you some good to be around other folk, get a routine, a job, socialize, and all that fun stuff."

"Yeah, I guess," said Matthew looking at the ground.

Though there were forty years difference between the two, Alex felt a feeling of not merely camaraderie but almost kinship with this boy swell in his heart. Though a wealth of differences between their own individual experiences existed, Alex remembered how miserable it felt to sit there four days sober with no one to turn to. That's why he had come in the first place. 'I'm gonna try my damnedest,' he thought. Matthew sat looking sad and scraggly. He looked across the interstitial space at Alex's face like he was a vulture that had come to pluck out his eyes.

"You did do your work, right?" Alex asked sternly.

"Yeah, I did."

"Good, I'm glad you didn't waste my time. Let's see it."

Matthew grabbed the spiral off the nightstand between them. He opened it up and held it out to Alex.

"Here it is," and fear began to envelop him.

Alex snatched the spiral and scanned it.

"Okay, we're gonna go line by line down your list. All I need from you is to answer my questions thoroughly and honestly."

Matthew nodded. There was a lump in his throat. He couldn't articulate it even if he had wanted to, but he did not intend to be completely truthful. At this point in his journey, he didn't have the capacity to be unyieldingly honest. It isn't that he wanted to lie or even planned to here but the propensity within him to avoid telling certain truths about himself was too great. Alex began to talk, and Matthew went into autopilot.

"So, I see the first name on here is your father. It says here and I quote 'physically, emotionally, and psychologically abused my mother. Took my sister from my mother. Lied to the cops to have my mother arrested. Spit all over my mother. Strategically abused my mom when I wasn't there to defend her. Told my mom to make everyone happy and kill herself,' and it looks like it goes on with all sorts of horrible things that he did to your mom but what about what he's personally done to you?"

"Those are personal," asserted Matthew.

"Right, they are. No one should have to go through what your mother and you went through. But everything here has to do with how he treated your mother. Is there any resentment you hold towards your father that solely pertains to yourself?"

"Yeah, he choked me. He's hit me and talked shit about me, and he called the cops on me."

"Okay, good. Now what have you done to him? You didn't put anything down."

"I haven't done anything to him."

"Matthew, I find that hard to believe. We've known each other a little while now and you're no saint. What have you done to him?"

"Nothing, that's just it."

"Hmm"

"Are you trying to justify my father's actions through my behavior? Don't victimize him!" Matthew nearly shouted.

"That's not what I'm trying to do Matthew. I'm trying to help you get to the root of why you do the things that you do by taking an in depth look at the dysfunctional relationships you've had throughout your life. It says here that 'he called the cops on you.' I'm sure he didn't do that for no reason."

"He called the cops on my mom for no reason all the time," Matthew quipped.

"Okay, but that's not what I asked. Why'd he do it then?"

"Because I hit him. I beat him up and I'm glad I did."

"Now why'd you do that?"

"Cuz he hit my mom."

They were only on the first name and they both felt as though they were already going in circles.

"Okay, let's take a step back from that," Alex began. "You know that you're not to blame for what your father did to your mother. You do know that right?"

"Yeah, but I should have protected her better." Matthew began to sniffle.

"Matthew, that's not your onus to carry. That's not your fault and it's thoughts and beliefs like that that drove you to drink and drug the way you did in the first place."

"I guess so," Matthew ostensibly conceded.

There was a brief pause between the two. Alex holding the spiral eyed Matthew while Matthew eyed the floor holding his hands. His eyes darted about the floor to avoid Alex's severe yet concerned gaze and he began to sweat. Fidgeting, Matthew cracked his fingers one by one across each hand. Alex sighed, gathering himself.

"Okay, the next name you put down is God. Let's see why you're upset with him. It says here 'is supposed to be omnipotent and wholly good but lets evil flourish. Let my father abuse my mom, lets my father live happily.' Did I miss anything?"

"No, that's about it," Matthew groaned resentfully.

"Matthew," Alex began by tossing the spiral on the bed. "You're a bright boy. What do you know about freewill?"

"Where do I begin?" he said, collecting himself both mentally and physically. He thought about the rosary on his neck and how it was meant to remind him that God was always to be with him. 'I'm not sure if I believe that anymore,' he thought.

"What I believe is… well first I gotta say that I don't know how I feel about God. I'm not sure if he exists. I don't hate him or deny that he could exist. But I guess I'm sorta indifferent to the whole thing. I believe in something though. I'm just not sure what."

Matthew paused, having forgotten that Alex's question had nothing to do with whether or not he believed in God.

"Right," said Alex. "All that's good and fine but I asked what you think of and how you feel about the idea of freewill?"

"Well, I think to believe in both God and free will is weak-minded. They say, 'oh God loves you, God can do anything,' said Matthew derisively in falsetto. But look at all the horrible shit that goes on in the world. I mean, pick a side; either God is in control of everything or he isn't. You can't claim there's an all-powerful being that so grandly deserves praise anytime something of minute decency happens yet blame people or the devil or general evil at hand when calamity occurs. I mean, where's your saintly superforce then?"

Matthew was more than content with his response. He hoped and arrogantly thought that that would shut Alex up about God.

"So, you said you believe in something, but it doesn't sound like you believe in freewill. Well, I hate to break it to you Mr. Semester-of-college-philosophy that there is both a God and freewill. I know that there's a God cuz I'm sittin here sober today and I know that I have freewill cuz I could get right on up and walk out this room and be done with you," he said while symbolically wiping his hands. "The reason I had asked you about this," he began again. "Is to see if you could come to terms with the idea that God didn't do those things to your mom. Your father's poor choice of freewill did. Can you get down with that conception?"

"Yeah, I guess."

Matthew sat stunned. It had been so easy to bash but he could live with this idea, not because God could now dwell in his heart but because it allowed him more ill-will to harbor towards his father. Matthew felt like a Judge. He had pardoned God while simultaneously augmenting his father's condemnation. 'I don't like this. I don't wanna argue through each and every one of these,' he thought. 'I'd rather budge and get this over with than have it go on for all eternity.'

"So… the next name here is Bella and you wrote that you 'treated her poorly.' What's the story there?"

"Well," started Matthew and he began to tell the story without reservation. He consciously told the truth and with Alex's skillful probing, downplaying of Matthew's part in the matter was averted. He was not ashamed of the abortion as he had once been.

As a planter cast seeds about a field not all of them take hold, and most not immediately. Matthew's mind lay spiritually fallow though seeds had been sown. There was no telling how long this seed, embedded with simple virtuous ideas, would lie dormant in the idle and morally barren fields of consciousness before the right conditions were present to enable germination. It is, of course, a possibility that the right combination of factors may never come and thus deny the seeds Alex sowed upon Matthew's psyche, during this process, a chance of ever taking root. But if his mind were to somehow become arable all that is needed to one day produce a great and sturdy oak is the propagation of a single seed. The odds were against the lot Alex had thrown and he knew this.

Alex read through every item on the list with careful analysis, with some Matthew told the truth, with others he omitted certain facts that would cast him in an unfavorable light. Honesty and falsehood, accuracy and distortion, humility and embellishment, omission and irrelevant details, so were the categorical responses that Matthew's answers arbitrarily took over the course of their eight-hour talk. By the end both were exhausted, Alex mentally, Matthew emotionally. Though Matthew had remained relatively standoffish and dishonest throughout the ordeal a vague sense of fulfillment came over him. He waited for Alex to get up and leave at any moment but instead he continued.

"So, Matthew, for this process to have its desired effect you need to be able to vocalize the most shameful and secretive parts of your past. I'm talking about the type of stuff that you'd plan to take to the grave with you. If you want to be truly free, if you want to no longer live as a slave to drugs and alcohol, you need to come clean about any dirty little secrets you may have. So, what have you not told me? What are you holding back?"

Matthew's head swirled. 'How could I ever tell anybody any of those things? I couldn't even be truthful about the stuff I did write down. No, he can't know any of that. No one can. Ever.' His mind raced to and fro and he shook at some of the thoughts. Sinister, horrible memories plagued him. Sexual, immoral, violent. 'No, no soul can ever know these things. Never. That's it. This is over. I'm done. But what about God? Does he know? Of course, he knows. So, if he knows, I don't have to tell anyone at all, especially Alex. If God knows, that's good enough for me. And if he knows everything, then he knows I'm sorry, and that I want to change, and that I love my mom, and that I would never do anything to hurt her, intentionally. God knows my heart, and I'm doing this for mom, and he knows that. But what if I start drinking and popping pills and snorting coke and meth again because I couldn't be honest now, and then I disappoint mom again, but next time it's worse? Does there have to be a next time? What did I even do this time? I have to find out. I'll ask Alex.' Alex had been sitting patiently.

"Well?"

"No, there's nothing else. I put everything down on that paper."

"Nothing," Alex said, giving Matthew some more time to think.

"Nope."

"Not even letting a goat lick your pecker when you were a kid or some weird shit like that?"

They heard a voice snicker out in the hall.

"Nope, nothin like that."

Okay then, I'm gonna need you to reflect on what we talked about for the next hour. Seriously think about if you left anything out. And then pray," Alex said, getting up to go.

"Okay, I can do that."

"I know you can, good job bud. I'm proud of you."

Alex turned to leave when Matthew said, "Wait, what did I do to my mom?"

Alex turned back around wide eyed.

"Well," he said. "You stole a bunch of her mom's shit and traded it to a crack dealer who then threatened to rape her when she tried to get it back or something along those lines."

Matthew could not believe it. Infinitesimal pieces of the incident started to come back to him hazily.

"Oh, okay," he said. "I was just wondering."

Alex walked out. Matthew rolled on his side to face the wall. He had missed dinner again but did not care. He wasn't hungry anyway. He fell asleep without doing any of the things Alex had told him to, and he laid, falling in and out of sleep, with his mind in a deep state of turmoil until morning.

<u>Part Two</u>

I

Matthew put his almost empty bowl of oatmeal in the dish area and went to step out in the gravel lot when Hugh pulled him aside and ushered him into the office.

"Sit down," he said. Matthew sat.

"Why didn't you go to any meetings last week?"

"Well, I've only been here about a week," responded Matthew.

"I looked right befo I called you in here. Today's your eleventh day. The four or so days you was on detox don't count but you been out the sick-room about a week now…exactly a week today in fact," Hugh rasped and cleared his throat.

"What you been doin all these days?" he continued.

"Walkin around lookin for a job."

"Any luck?"

"Not yet."

"Well, you got nineteen days paid up. But even when you find a job you gon have to make you two weekly meetings. So, you better find a way to start getting them in."

Matthew did not like being chided but there was something so good-natured in Hugh that it did not bother him.

"I know."

"What type of work you lookin fo?"

"Restaurant work."

"You eva done anything clerical?"

"Like office work?"

"Yeah, like office work. Filing papers, filling out forms, answerin phones. You know, that sorta thing," said Hugh.

"No, I haven't done any of that, but I could."

"I bet you could," Hugh rasped. "We need some young blood in here. Trim the deadwood, you know what I'm sayin."

Matthew did not know what to say.

"Between you and me," Hugh started up again. "We might have an opening on staff soon. Right here at the front desk. But don't tell nobody I said that. You don't want no competition and it ain't a sure thing. Now go on out and find some work. I'll look out for you."

"Thank you," and Matthew rose to leave.

"Oh, and make yo damn meetings," rasped Hugh as he lit a cigarette.

"Yessir."

Matthew stepped out onto the sidewalk and looked at the glittering downtown skyscrapers that protruded magnificently about a mile north of where he stood. 'I might try and go find some work there,' he thought. The past week he had headed south applying for jobs around the Texas Medical Center. As Matthew stood facing the shimmering metropolis, he couldn't believe he hadn't tried his luck in the city's jeweled center of industry and culture.

Lost in thought, he ventured north mesmerized by the sun bouncing back off this modern mountain range. 'The symbol of all human progress, and I'll be working there. I could valet. Rich people would throw me the keys to their cars, or I could wait on sophisticated people at a five-star restaurant and make big tips. Men with women much too beautiful for them would slap hundreds down on polished tables to pay for their overpriced wine and tell me to keep the change. I'll be able to…'

While lost in thought, a white Mercedes ran through a red

light as he was crossing the street. It slammed on its brakes screeching to a stop a few feet from Matthew. A well-dressed man with slicked back hair leaned out the driver's side window and yelled, "Get out the fucking road before I beat the living shit out of you." His beautiful female passenger yelled, "move retard," and snickered. Matthew stood frozen. The car sped around him; a middle finger lifted out the sunroof.

Still in the middle of the street, heart thumping, Matthew looked up past the skyscrapers now directly overhead, and thanked God for sparing him. He moved to the sidewalk. A man in a suit smoking a cigarette looked at him.

"You alright? That guy was a dick," he said.

"Yeah, I'm fine," Matthew managed to say with teeth chattering. "Hey, how much to bum a smoke?"

"Do I look like a nigger?" asked the businessman.

"What?" Matthew was taken aback.

"Am I black?"

"Uh…no," said Matthew confused.

"Then I ain't gonna charge you," said the businessman handing him a cigarette and a lighter.

"Uh, thanks," Matthew walked off puffing and shaking his head. He aimlessly winded through the massive buildings.

'Where could I work,' he thought.

Stepping into a pizzeria, he asked if they were hiring.

"Yeah, drivers," said the fat manager. "You gotta car?"

"No, I don't."

"Bike?"

Matthew shook his head no.

"Then move around, I'm trying to do business."

Matthew went to walk out the door but stopped and turned around.

"What about cashiers or cooks?" he asked.

"What the hell did I just say? I said I need drivers. What are you stupid?"

"No, I ain't stupid," said Matthew walking out.

Walking a block west Matthew sat on an empty bench dejected. 'I oughtta go back and slap the shit outta that fat motherfucker. Oh, what's the use? I still wouldn't have a job.' He looked up and watched fast floating clouds pass over the building tops. 'What's gonna happen if I don't have rent money in nineteen days? Is Hugh gonna kick me out? Would mom take me back?' A roar of laughter brought his vision back down to street view. A group of women and men, probably in their thirties, sat at a posh restaurant patio across the street drinking wine and cocktails. 'God, that looks nice. What I wouldn't do to do something like that. Wait, when have I ever done something like that? I chug malt liquor and smash the bottle. Not sit around and drink fruity cocktails. Fucking lame-os. I need to do something with my life, but I don't want to be like those losers with a sweater tied around my shoulders and colorful short shorts and designer sunglasses. It isn't even that bright out. At least they get to drink.'

As Matthew thought this, a man wearing a reflective work-vest was walking towards him and clearly looking at him. He was black and baldheaded probably in his late fifties.

"You that new boy at the Home ain't you?"

"Yeah, I'm Matthew. You live there?"

"I'm George, and yeah I do." He chuckled, showing a single tooth in the front of his mouth.

"What ya doin down here?" he continued.

"I was hoping to find work, but most places say they don't need anybody or all they need is delivery drivers. You work for the city?"

"Yeah, I usually just walk around downtown most days changin the bags outta the trash cans. I can see about getting you put on. I'll have to ask the bossman though."

"Okay, yeah. If you could, I'd appreciate it." Matthew's spirits began to lift. "Hey, what time is it?"

"Oh," George said looking at his watch. "Almost eleven. I'ma get lunch in about a half hour if you wanna join?"

"I would but I don't have any money."

"That's alright, I wouldn't do this for just anyone, but you seem like good people. How bout you buy me some food sometime when you find work. Sound fair?"

"Yeah, sounds good to me. Thanks."

"Ok, well I gotta change a few more bins. Wanna walk with me and keep me company for a minute then we'll grab something?"

"Sure."

George was not as old as he moved or maybe he just didn't seem that old. As he shuffled along the sidewalk, he spoke to Matthew, and Matthew responded but not fully taking in what he said. Matthew's faculties were focused on the concrete landscape around them and the bizarre scenes it held with each passing corner. A homeless woman sitting up against a building winked at him while George changed out a bag. Across the street, two homeless men, twacked out of their minds on kush, yelled out from a concrete ledge to pedestrians walking by a few feet below.

"Lesbians and thespians gather round. The government is a reptilian race."

"Ted Cruz has a zipper down his back that he uses to slide into his human skin."

"Be weary of these shifters young traveler," the first said, indicating Matthew.

'At least I'm not that crazy,' thought Matthew. And he thought about the time he had been awake on meth for about a week and ate a bunch of sleeping pills, but the meth was too powerful, and he just hallucinated instead of sleeping. He had seen lizards of all sizes around his house with two-dimensional cartoon characters mocking him and every time he went to grab one it would jump into a picture just out of his reach and taunt him. His mom was worried trying to figure out what he had taken as he sat there talking about hippie drum circles and chameleons that would not stop biting his ear lobes. 'Thank

God I'm not that crazy,' he thought again.

"Here we are," George said, stopping in front of a deli.

Inside George ordered them two ham sandwiches and went to wash his hands. Matthew sat twiddling his fingers anxiously. When George returned, he struck up a simple conversation, and the two got to know each other. It was the scene of a great friendship forging.

Leaving the deli, Matthew was tired. He didn't feel like walking the mile back to the halfway house, and so he went to the nearest light-rail station to hitch a ride. A train was coming, and he pretended to purchase a ticket at a kiosk. The train pulled up and he took a seat. As it glided south, he wondered if perhaps he could find a better area to work than downtown. Two stops later, Matthew stepped out onto the platform. A clock at the station read 1:07 p.m. 'Two more hours before I can go inside and rest my head,' he thought. 'What should I do? I could go to a meeting. No, I'll do that tomorrow.' Matthew walked to the side of 1083 and into the Serenity Garden. The shaded area was wonderful. Wind blew the Spanish moss that hung from the Live Oak. Magnolia, bamboo, crepe myrtle, and hibiscus encircled him. Sitting at a wooden table he took his shoes off and felt the soft grass beneath his feet. Resting his head on the table he thought of his mom. He loved her and wanted to be at her side. 'I'd do anything to go back home.' Closing his eyes in the luscious verdancy, a distant police siren lulled him to sleep.

II

That night after dinner, Hugh called Matthew over to give him a letter that had been dropped off for him. Excited and extremely nervous, Matthew was almost certain that it was from his mother. He had left her several messages but as far as he knew she was still very hurt and angry or else she would have answered. He would rather have her yell at him than not answer but would rather she not answer than for him to have to hear her cry. That is what tore at his heart. The thought of her alone and sad, especially that she was alone and sad because of him. Matthew's hand holding the letter shook. He asked Hugh for a cigarette and then stepped out to read it in privacy. In the alley, Matthew lit the cigarette and tore open the envelope. It was typed and dated from the day prior. His mother would not have typed a letter. It read:

3/26/13

Hi Matthew,

I'm glad you are getting the help you deserve, and think you are in the right place to get some help.

I know it's not easy what you are going through. Even though our relationship has been poor the past 3 years, I would someday like to be part of your life again. If there is

anything I can do to help with your current situation, just
let me know – rent money at the Men's Home, etc…
Also, I know you probably would not take me up on this
offer, but you are welcome to stay at my place after you
leave the Men's Home. I'm wanting to leave Houston in the
next few months, and maybe a change like that would do
you some good as well.
Anyway, I love you very much despite our past differences.
Love
Dad

At first Matthew was angry. 'He doesn't love me, or he would
have never treated mom and me the way he did. How could
he ever think I'd live with him, let alone move away? That
motherfucker. He's just trying to steal me from mom. Just like
he did with my sister. This isn't about wanting to help me. This
is an attempt to hurt her further. He's trying to hurt her by
getting to me during a rift. What a piece a shit. I didn't think I
would hear from him. It has been about a week since I called.
Why did he say to 'let him know' if he could help? That's the
whole reason I called. Does he just want me to humble myself
again? He probably doesn't trust giving me money. That bastard.
How could he ever think I would want a relationship with him?
That smug asshole. I don't want him in my life. I can't believe I
reached out in the first place. Did I betray mom again? I don't
need a dad. I have gotten along just fine without him. Up until
now me and mom have done just fine.

But Matthew did want a father. Deep down he knew that.
But it made him rage to think so. So, he always pushed that
thought down, and buried it deep within his heart's recesses.
He conceded to himself occasionally that yes, he did want a
father, just not his father. But he knew this to be untrue also
and it made him even more wrathful to think that he wanted his
father to be his father. However, none of this was conscious in
Matthew at the moment. The wind blew. His head swirled. All
he knew was that he wanted to call his mom.

Matthew went inside to see Dan at the front desk. He always dreaded asking to call his mother at the front desk. He was not sure he could keep it together if she answered. But he would rather lose his composure and hear her voice than ostensibly keep it together with overwhelming feelings of not being loved and uncertainty tormenting him. So, he asked.

"Hey, Super Dan, can I make a call?"

"Yeah, sure. Go for it."

He picked up the phone and dialed the number. It rang.

"Hello," his mother's sweet voice said apprehensively.

"Hey, mom. I didn't think you'd answer. I love you mom. I miss you."

Matthew only heard a sigh, and his mother's continued but slow breath on the other end.

"Mom, are you there? Are you okay?"

"No, Matthew I'm not okay."

"Mom, I'm sorry for whatever I did. I don't even remember it."

"I didn't think you would. You know, that just makes it all the worse. The hell you can put me through and not even remember it."

"Mom, I wasn't in my right mind. I'm sorry."

"When are you in your right mind?" she asked rhetorically.

"I never meant to hurt you. I'm so sorry mom. Please forgive me," Matthew pleaded.

"I just can't do that right now. Between you and your father, I have had just about enough. You can't beat a dead horse." Matthew thought of Raskolnikov.

"Mom, I'm not like him. I'm sorry. I'll change."

"No, Matthew, you're not like him. You used to be such a sweet boy. Whatever happened? You're always on those fucking pills and when you mix them with alcohol, you're ten times worse. No, you're not like him but you hurt me and that's the same," and she sobbed full force.

"Mom, I'm sorry, please forgive me. I'll never hurt you again."

"With the path you're on now, I don't believe that. I can't have you around here right now. You're out of control. You need to get your act together."

"When can I come home, mom? I love you. I miss you. I'm sorry."

"I don't know but you're going to have to figure something out because you are not coming back here until you get some help."

"But mom, I miss you. I'm sorry."

"Well, you're going to have to get stronger."

There was a long pause.

"I can't do this right now. You have no idea of the toll you are taking on me. I have to go."

There was a click.

"Mom, are you there? I love you. Mom, please forgive me."

Matthew hung up the phone. There was a physical pang in his heart. Tears streamed down his face. He turned around and went out the door. Dan said something but Matthew couldn't hear it.

Stepping into the cool city night, Matthew sat down on the stoop of the building next door, the meeting-hall. The wind blew and his thoughts raced. 'God, if you're real please let my mom forgive me. I'll do anything, spread your word, feed the hungry, tend to the sick, practice abstinence, whatever you want.' The tears no longer streamed from his eyes but remained on his face. He licked what he could of them and wept quietly but bitterly.

The door behind him swung open. A man he couldn't identify because the light inside was directly behind him looked down at him and said, "hey, old boy. We about to have a meeting in here if you wanna come on in and get you some solution. Might help with whatever you going through."

"George, is that you?"

"Of course, it's me. Who'd you think it was?" he said, chuckling through his mostly toothless mouth.

"I don't know. I couldn't tell who it was," said Matthew,

getting up and following George inside and taking a seat next to him.

The man speaking reminded Matthew of a Southern Baptist preacher. His intonation, elocution, and fervency certainly mirrored one. He wore a white dress shirt with a slim black tie. Matthew noticed that many people were in business attire.

It was hot. The room was crowded. Sweat trickled on his forehead and temples. Yellow underarm spots showed when he thrust his arms up gesticulating violently. Other people sweated too and nodded their heads in approval to what the recovery evangelist proclaimed. Three well-dressed women sat in the corner, hats concealing most of their faces. Their smooth ebony legs and full busts beckoned Matthew. He tried to focus on the sermonizing, but his attention kept being called back to the way they seductively fanned themselves. Matthew shook his head in an attempt to remove his libidinousness. 'I have to concentrate on what these people are talking about so that mom will eventually let me come home.'

"See I never thought of myself as an alcoholic," the man standing said. "You see, I like to smoke crack. I use drugs alcoholically. And there ain't no other way to smoke crack than to smoke it like a damn fiend. You know what I'm saying," he said pointing to a bald and toothless man in the front row who then nodded in obsequence. Several *mm-hmms* rang in from around the room. Everyone sat in complete deference to the authority in this man's voice and the message that it carried. "I used to wake up the day after payday with no money, not a dolla. And see I had a good job too. But come 4:30 Friday, I start thinkin of ways to relax. How 'm I gon relax? I'd say, 'I think I'm gon get me a couple Schlitz malt liquor bulls,'" and he chuckled. "Y'all remember them Schlitz malt liquor bulls." *Mm-hmms* poured in again. "Except fo maybe you," and he pointed at Matthew. Matthew grew flush.

"No difference though," he continued. "This illness knows no economic boundaries, races, colors, creeds. But let me tell ya. Bout 4:30 each Friday, I'd start thinkin that I deserved to relax. You know what I'm talkin about," and he pointed to Hugh and laughed. "Just stop and get me a lil something on the way home from a hard day's work to take the edge off. So, I'd go on to the sto, get me a couple of them Schlitz malt liquor bulls. I thought I deserved it right. But after I crack one of those bad boys open, and soon as it hits my lips, I start thinkin about some crack-cocaine. You pickin up what I'm putting down?" he said pointing to someone else. "I'd say, 'I think I might just go and get me a lil twenty,' just a lil twenty," he repeated mocking himself. "So, after damn but just one Schlitz malt liquor bull, I shoot for the crack house. Like boom, off to the races. Gon get me some of that yella crack. Pick me up a lil twenty. Next thing I know, It's Monday morning, I ain't got no money. Just been paid, need I remind ya. I'm with some woman, don't know her name. All I know is she ain't my wife. And I'm fixin to be late for work. You smell what I'm steppin in?" he asked the room. "I'd work hard all week long. Then Friday come and I thought I could use a little break. And I'd be stuck in that same hellacious cycle still now if I didn't humble myself to ask another man for help and follow his suggestions to a T. This ain't no buffet style program, take what you want and leave the rest. You gotta do all of it. See, I thought I was a recreational crack smoker," and he slapped his knee in laughter. "Cuz, I only smoked on the weekends. Not knowin, I was a full-blown crackhead. We can keep the chaos up a long time. It becomes normal for us. Cuz we so sick that all we can see is the next hit, drink, pill or whatever it is you do that got you sittin in this room right now."

Matthew had been listening intently but here his attention began to fade. He thought of his mother sorrowfully, and his father distastefully. 'I'll do anything to earn her trust back.' His thoughts fluttered about for the remainder of the meeting. He snapped back to consciousness when everyone stood up in a circle and went to hold hands. Matthew wanted to go hold one of the women's hands but didn't want to make it obvious.

Matthew took George's and another man's hand, closed his eyes, and followed along in the Lord's Prayer. Mid-prayer, he opened his eyes to glimpse the women's faces. He stood appalled. "Give us this day our daily bread." Matthew discerned their rigid jaw-lines, Adam's apples, and contrived hyperfemininity. 'How could I have been attracted to… I would. I wonder… the inside of their mouths, their gums, tongues, throat,' and his penis stirred. "and lead us not into temptation but deliver us from evil, amen."

Flustered, Matthew quickly said, "see you later" to George and left. He headed for 1083 around the corner. His head whirled. The wind blew passed him upon his back. 'What the fuck is going on with me?' Dread and fierce motherly devotion swirled along with paternal ambivalence and sexual confusion. He walked into 1083, passed everyone, and went to bed dismayed.

III

That night Matthew dreamt that he just received his pilot's license and took his mom on a celebratory flight. As they took to the sky it was as beautiful as a day could get. His mother sat to his right and beamed with delight and pride in the young man her son was becoming. Matthew maneuvered the aircraft nimbly. He would ascend steeply and then abruptly tilt the aircraft forward. This momentarily left them with a sense of weightlessness and each time they laughed gleefully. Everything was perfect. As far as they were concerned, they were the only two people in the world. Occasionally, mild turbulence interrupted the placidity of his somewhat reckless yet pleasurable aerial stroll but never too harshly nor for too long. In the distance, they could see the white, wispy, fluffy, cottonlike, cumulus clouds transition into sternly foreboding nimbostratus with heaps of sinisterly ominous cumulonimbus hovering atop. "I'm gonna steer clear of there," yelled Matthew. Swallowing anxiously, his mother nodded approvingly and screamed, "It'd be wise if you did." But upon turning left, Matthew realized they were walled in on three sides by these dark and dense storm clouds. A moment before everything had been so cerulean but now his mother pointed toward the quickly closing stretch of semi blue sky. As they sped towards it, torrential rain gushed from the heavens. Thunder cracked. Lightning flashed. The blissful flight on a splendid afternoon that they so recently shared had been cruelly snatched by Zeus in an instant. Signal was lost on both the radio and GPS. 'Where am I taking us? Why can't I just land safely like everyone else? Who else would make their mother endure such chaos? Why do I insist on terrorizing her?' Just as Matthew was making his final attempt to wrest control of the plane and the situation the motor malfunctioned. The cockpit's electronics went haywire. The engine sputtered. They tail-spun into the abyss.

Since Matthew had gotten off detox and moved into 1083, he began to meet and befriend a few of the forty some odd people who lived in that building along with some that lived in the complex's other houses, like George. There was Lester a middle-aged black man with a moustache originally from Las Vegas, who had the bed next to Matthew's. Lester had tried to help Matthew out one day with some cigarette money, so he offered Matthew five bucks to take an old toothbrush with some bleach, water, and rag to his beat-up old Airforce Ones. Matthew scrubbed and scrubbed but they didn't come out as clean as Lester had wanted. He reluctantly paid him anyway though.

There was a white guy who looked and talked exactly like Mo Green from *The Godfather* who just came down from Wyoming. His name was Dan, and he was pissed to find out that the Men's Home had bed bugs. When he found out he said, "fuck this man. I'm outta here," to no one in particular. He got up amid the tiny, yet packed smoke-filled smoke-room. Dan was well liked but no one even budged. An annoyingly arrogant crackhead named Tim walked through with a towel around his waist, smoke clinging to his freshly showered pale body and slicked back hair and said, "shut up, you ain't goin nowhere. You're fuckin broke like the rest of us. Where you gonna go?" "I am too," Dan responded proudly. "I don't know but I'll figure it out," and left. He didn't even bother to grab all his worldly possessions which were two black garbage bags filled with clothes because they were probably infested. No one ever saw Dan again.

Tim had gotten there after his wife kicked him out for pawning their car to the dope man. He didn't look like a crackhead until he opened his mouth. It just so happened that the crack dealer Tim had traded his car to was also there getting help. He was a black guy named Jason who was bright-skinned, covered in tattoos, and always wore a wave cap. Tim pleaded with Jason to sell him his car back so his wife would let him back in the house.

"You ain't even got the money," said Jason.

"But I will. Let me have the car and I'll give you half of every one of my paychecks until it's paid for."

"Motherfucker still sound high. Promisin some shit he ain't even got yet."

"But I will. I'm about to get my job back. You gotta believe me."

"Motherfucker ain't even got a job," said Jason chuckling.

"Matter fact," Jason continued. "You still owe me bout fo hunid for the that last sack of rocks I gave you. That's why I took yo car you fuckin crackhead." Jason stood up for effect and smacked the back of his hand on his palm a few times. "You lucky I don't change the title."

"You're lucky I don't call the cops."

"Like they'd believe yo crackhead ass. You still smell like brillo." The smoke-room erupted in laughter.

"Like they'd believe you with your rap sheet."

"At least I can form a sentence half the time."

"Not when you're barred out." Matthew's brain had instantly lit up and he felt hot. "You think you're some big dealer, but you're passed out half the time."

"Don't say I ain't bout my money, cuz I got yo ride, don't I? If you ain't bout money, then get the fuck up from around me. Go ahead and eat a dick while you at it. You lucky I don't tell yo wife how you be fuckin them nasty hoes while you smokin at my spot."

Tim stormed out exasperated while Jason had relaxed and lit another cigarette. Little scenes such as this happened all the time. Not all were heated but scenes, nonetheless. Characters of all sorts came through. Somebody was always either coming or going, and if someone was on their way out it was almost always because they had violated some rule or relapsed and not because they were able to get financially stable, get on their feet, and move out for a better life. There was a revolving door, most people ended back up on the street and usually weren't heard from again or crawled back in in an even more pathetic and pitiful condition than when they arrived the first time.

Matthew started to get along just fine with everyone. Old, young, middle-aged, black, white, Hispanic; people looked out for him. He seemed to remind many of them of themselves when they were younger. Not in appearance but how he carried himself. He was rough around the edges but noticeably kind at heart. Matthew had also begun to find that keeping up a tough façade could be exhausting. It was a defensive strategy and he soon learned that there was nothing to be afraid of. So, he dropped it.

Matthew quickly became one of the most well-known and popular guys around the Home. Most of the guys sympathized and commiserated with him about the pain they had heard he had caused his mother. Many of them had done similar things and wanted to live vicariously by seeing him successfully return home and do things a "kid" his age would be told he should be doing, like going to college. The most common piece of advice that people seemed to bestow upon Matthew though was "get this now and save yourself some heartache." They all seemed to revel in the thought of what if they had gotten sober when they were twenty or thirty or fifty years younger, at Matthew's age.

No matter how well he was liked, Matthew still had to work. The next morning at breakfast, a short, rotund, mustached, middle-aged, black man named Jerry asked if anyone needed work and said if they did to ride the train with him there that morning. Matthew took him up on his offer. It wasn't until they were on the train that Matthew thought to ask about the job.

"So, what kind of place is this?"

"It's a linen service," said Jerry.

As the light-rail rolled south, Matthew stared out the window at downtown Houston moving further away as the neglected Astrodome grew closer.

IV

The doors opened. Jerry hastily stepped off without saying anything. Matthew thought he could have at least said something, but he also didn't realize it was the last stop and that he had to get off since the train had run out of track. He caught up to Jerry whose speedy stride swung the plump little man's sinewy hips swiftly along. A prostitute walked by after what appeared to be a long night.

"It's about seven-forty now. We gotta be clocked in by eight."

"Are we almost there?" Matthew kept up with not nearly as much effort.

"Yeah, it's just right up the road."

The two moved along, one walking, the other power walking down an industrial road lined with beverage bottling plants, mostly beer. Matthew thought about what it'd be like to sneak into one and hide out in a closet or behind a door or under a desk until they closed up and then going to town. They moved along towards a cul-de-sac.

"What time these places close up?"

"Oh, they all close about the same time round five or sex." Jerry shook his head. "I mean six," he corrected himself. "You prolly won't be here that long though it's your first day. You gotta do paperwork and all that."

"What time does the train stop runnin?"

"Not till after midnight. Why?" Jerry looked at Matthew sideways with an eyebrow raised as they strode along. Matthew looked spellbound at the plants.

"Just wonderin," he said absentmindedly. "Hey, you gotta cigarette?"

"Yeah," said Jerry begrudgingly. "We gotta hurry up though."

"Thanks," said Matthew taking a loosey and a lighter from Jerry, lighting it, drawing it to get it going, almost pocketing the lighter, shaking his head upon realizing the mistake that Jerry silently pointed out, returning the transparent-green, half-filled lighter with the safety removed and the flame turned all the way up to its rightful owner, forcefully puffing the inchoately lit cigarette once more to ensure a quality and well-rounded burn, suavely transferred it back to his right hand, and turned to continue the conversation in one smooth natural motion and seamless rhythm without skipping a beat all in a few of seconds.

"So, what are we gonna do?"

"Well," he began looking off into the distance. "I'll probably be upstairs either folding or sorting but you'll prolly be downstairs at the loading dock. It's steady work but when you done you done and can leave." Matthew's eyesight remained fixed on Jerry whose head seemed as if on a swivel that pivoted back and forth. "Whereas I gotta stay to six o'clock irregardless. I wish they'd move me to over where you gonna be at. Y'all can take y'all's time and go at your own speed." He said, shaking his head in what seemed to be disbelief at Matthew's unearned serendipity. "However fast y'all go sets the pace for the whole operation. Man, I wish I was at where you probably gonna be," he threw in superfluously while shifting his bodyweight continuously between his two chunky legs. "I can't even understand what these little old Spanish ladies be sayin to me. I bet they sho like you though, young white boy with blue eyes oo-wee."

'Something's up. He's overselling this. How does he know where I'll be?' Matthew thought.

"My eyes are green," said Matthew suspiciously.

"So, fucking what?" Jerry said jokingly. "Blue, green, same difference," he said laughing. "All y'all white boys look the same anyway." He patted Matthew playfully on the abdomen with the back of his hand. "Anyway," he continued. "It's about eight now. You go on inside to the office right there and get a punch card, and I'll be in and see," and Jerry walked around the corner and out of sight.

'What the fuck is he up to? It doesn't matter. I need the money,' he thought wonderingly.

Matthew stepped out of the brightly lit and already surprisingly warm morning and into a dingy lobby artificially lit yellow. He stood for a minute taking it all in, bracing himself for what was to come. He looked down at the heavily scuff marked tile floor. When he looked up a woman was standing there.

"Hi, can I help you?" she said.

She was Hispanic, about thirty and voluptuous, dressed business casual in a blouse, pencil skirt, heels, and no ring. She wore an expression that said, 'don't waste my time.' Matthew was both attracted and intimidated. He didn't know what to say.

"Are you lost or stupid?"

"Neither. I'm here for work," he declared, having suddenly found the words.

"Well it doesn't work like that. You have to apply, and we'll call you to set up an interview if we like what we see."

"Well, I was told y'all needed help, so I came because I need money."

"Who told you we needed help?"

"This guy Jerry."

"Is he here? He's not clocked in yet, but he sends some..." she seemed flustered in an attempt to find the workplace appropriate term. "Kid," she finally answered.

"I don't know where he is."

"Okay, well the fact is today we are short staffed, and Jerry's not here for the loading dock, slowing up the whole process. So, there's that. Come in," she motioned Matthew into her office. "The sooner I get you into the system, the sooner I can do my actual job."

Matthew sat in a piss-yellow, partially cracked hard-plastic chair across from a particle board desk disheveled with paperwork. An artificial plant stood in the corner with a saucer underneath it. On the wall, to his right was a kitsch painting of a bowl of fruit. On his left were two inspirational posters; one was of an Arctic fox against a dark snowy background and said *fortitude*, the other was of a gopher sticking its head out of its burrow with the sun gleaming behind it and said *bravery*. Matthew thought they were dumb but was oddly attracted to their messages. The walls to Matthew's sides were covered in a faux brick wallpaper, and the floor was laminate. She sat down in a rickety office chair that before sitting down, Matthew had noticed the seat was torn and the foam was starting to come out. There was a plastic bowl at the edge of her desk filled with change. Matthew's attention was drawn to the quarters in that bowl, but he couldn't figure out why.

"So, I am Esperanza Mendoza. I'm the facility manager. And you are?"

"Matthew Wilkinson," he said, not making eye contact but instead mysteriously eyeing the coins.

She clicked a pen and started to write on a form. Two windows displayed the Astrodome in disrepair behind her. 'Years ago, Astroworld must have been right around here. That was so much fun. That's when being a kid was fun. When did the amusement stop? For the park, it must have been 05 or 06. But for me…,' he sat stumped for a minute while Ms. Mendoza silently filled out some paperwork. 'Actually, about the same time,' he figured. 'I was in third grade when I learned dad beat mom. No more fun for me after that. Must have been all I learned that year. At least I wasn't alone in losing out on the fun. It stopped for the whole city that year. Being alone in joylessness isn't any better but we still often seek to avoid it. But

I guess someone else already figured that out. Plus, the city had its people. And I wasn't alone either, I had mom and she had me. Oh, mom…' Matthew wanted to cry but wouldn't allow himself to tear up. Ms. Mendoza felt a weird shift in his mien all of a sudden.

"Birthday?"

"April 20th, 1994."

"God, you're so young," she remarked. "What are you eighteen, nineteen? What are you doing here?"

"I need money."

"What about your folks? They need you to help out, don't they?"

"I don't want to talk about it."

"Kicked out huh? Drug problem is it?" She judgmentally eyed Matthew's clothes. "Well don't get hurt on the job. Even if you could pass a drug test, you're not going to be getting anything."

"What other questions are on that form?" said Matthew, growing perturbed.

"Address?"

"Umm, it's at the corner of Fannin and Alabama. I can't think of the numbers."

"That's okay, you do have a home where you're staying at though don't you?"

"Yes."

"That's all I need to know about that then. Transportation?"

"I took the light-rail here," she jotted something down.

"Social?"

"Not really."

"No," she chuckled. "Social security number."

"I have no idea. Is that going to be an issue?"

"No, between me and you, most of the people here don't have one."

The door in the lobby opened. Matthew felt a presence fill the doorway behind him. Spinning around he saw Jerry. His jaw was clenched. The expression on his face said, 'Keep quiet. Don't say a word.' His eyes reiterated the message. He knocked lightly and in a friendly pattern on the doorframe. Ms. Mendoza looked up.

"It's about time you got here," she said sharply.

"Yeah, I'm sorry ma'am. I was runnin late."

"Well, don't let it happen again."

Matthew wondered what he was up to.

"So, I decided to have... what was it... Matthew?" He nodded. "on loading dock today, and I guess I'll have Leonella show you how to fold and sort. I shouldn't reward your tardiness, but I can't start Matthew there. It doesn't work like that. So, go upstairs and tell her that I sent you to learn, okay?"

"Yessum, thank you." And he briskly left.

'That bastard, he cheated me. How did he know?'

"I'll fill in the rest of your paperwork. It's not much," she said and turned and bent over away from Matthew to place a form in a file cabinet. Matthew stared at her delicious figure from behind. She finished, picked up a set of keys on her desk and said, "Come with me."

Matthew followed her down a hallway watching her hips swing in the business attire. A single door stood at the end of the hall. The exit sign above it flickered ominously. "Raul is in charge of the loading dock. Listen to what he says. You'll get a thirty-minute lunch break at 11:30 and you'll probably be finished by about 4:30 or 5. Any questions?"

"When can I expect a paycheck?"

"A little quick to that, aren't we? You'll be on the next cycle that goes out. Anything else?" She paused before the door. "No," he said, not satisfied with her first response and so didn't bother asking another.

She opened the door to a covered outside area with rolling blue bins everywhere that were filled with clear trash bags that were filled themselves with what looked like blankets. Ms. Mendoza still held the door open, leaning forward, arm outstretched while Matthew obliviously took the scene in. Trucks were backed up to ramps loading and unloading more bags. Two men stood at a conveyor belt grabbing bags out of the bins, cutting them open and throwing the contents onto the belt that went up at a forty-five-degree angle into a hole in the ceiling. "Well, here you are. That's Raul in the red," she said, pointing to a Latino man facing the other way with the H-town star tattooed on the back of his head visible through a low-fade. The man facing Raul got his attention, and he turned around pointing to himself to ask if he were needed. Ms. Mendoza shook her head no but then twinkled her fingers in a flirtatious wave and scrunched up her face in a friendly smile. She then nudged Matthew out the door, and he heard it click closed behind him. None of the visual scenery that he was trying to absorb could compare to the foul stench that permeated the place. Raul came up.

"Who are you?"

"I'm the new guy, Matthew."

"Well alright then, let's get to work," and he headed back to the conveyor. Matthew followed. At the belt, Raul started grabbing bags and with an unsheathed box-cutter between his fingers cut a semi-circle into the bag and flung it forward while holding onto it and thereby scattering dirty sheets onto the belt system.

"This is Chuy," Matthew nodded. Chuy had a completely shaved head, a baby face with an incipient mustache, and eyebrow slits. He was just a few years older than Matthew. He nodded back.

"You ever done anything like this?" asked Raul.

"No."

"What have you done before?"

"The only official job I've had was at McDonald's."

"Motherfucker said McDonald's," interjected Chuy who while he laughed displayed brilliantly white teeth. Raul chuckled. "Well this is gonna be different. This is gon work you. What about unofficially?"

"I don't wanna talk about it."

"I bet that motherfucker be slangin."

Raul tilted his head inquiringly.

"I used to but not no more."

"I told you fool. Them white boys, if they do it right, make a killin. Sellin fifteen and twenty-dollar grams and shit to their rich little friends. "You rich fool?"

"If I was rich would I be here?"

"He's got a point," said Raul.

"I bet you fool he be doin el pase."

"Well, do you?"

"I used to but not no more."

Raul picked up from the previous conversation. "It don't make no difference if he hasn't done this type of work. Hell, that's a good thing. Mean I don't have to reteach him the right way. Well, go on over there and grab you a blade off the fuse-box," he said pointing. Matthew grabbed a chipped and rusty box-cutter and returned.

"So, you see, just grab a bag like me and cut like this," directed Raul. Matthew took a bag and clumsily sliced into it and awkwardly threw the sheets out which almost didn't make it onto the belt. "No, not like that," said Chuy. "Cut like you gon cut a smiley face into a fool you don't like." "Alright," said Matthew, doing it to perfection. Chuy nodded approvingly. They went along for a minute.

"Why's does it smell like fuckin shit in here?" Matthew soon asked.

"All these bags are filled with dirty linens from the Med Center. Some of them are covered with piss and shit and vomit and blood. You gotta be careful not to have any of them touch you. It's really nasty," said Raul

"I had noticed some stains but hadn't put it together. Shouldn't we be wearing gloves and face masks and goggles or some type of protective gear?"

"We used to have all that. But they said they did some tests and found that the stuff we're handling really isn't that toxic. I don't know. I think they really just don't want to pay for that stuff. You know, cut costs wherever they can."

Matthew took the side of the belt next to Raul, cutting open bags and dispersing their contents on the line. The three worked in silence for a few minutes with only the sound of the conveyor system heard. Chuy was the first to speak.

"¿Que piensas?"

"Sí, es bueno para ser güero."

"Me vale madre que sea güero, nadamas me importa que trabaje duro."

"Ahuevo, estoy de acuerdo."

Matthew knew they were talking about him. He knew güero but he didn't hear any inflammatory language and so he didn't care. He could understand some of what was said. He spent a lot of time around various Spanish speakers growing up. Though he didn't often disclose to people immediately that he could follow, for the most part, what was being said. He didn't want to offend anyone. He often thought it condescending when white people chose to speak subpar Spanish to someone who probably speaks English. At least better English than their lousy Spanish. 'Why do white people just assume that they don't speak English? I'm fucking mortified when someone slows down their speech because they think that'll help someone understand. Why are people so quick to let Hispanic people know they speak broken Spanish and then clown them for speaking broken English?' Matthew also didn't want to overplay his hand right away in case he was able to hear something he shouldn't have been able to comprehend through feigned ignorance. But if he came out with the fact that he understood a fair deal of conversation too late, he'd be pegged for an eavesdropper. So, he just kept his head down and worked like it didn't concern him.

The monotony of the work became mechanical. It allowed him to drift off in his head and to think about his mom. He tried to put the pieces together. 'Alex said I stole some of mom's stuff that belonged to grandma. But what?' He tried to reach back in his mind, but it was a brick wall. Alcohol and alprazolam had done a number on his memory. 'I never steal from mom. What could I have taken? What would I have taken? Did she get it back? I can't believe Leo threatened to rape her. I'm gonna kill that motherfucker. So, help me god. I'm gonna shoot him in the fucking face. For some reason, I remember my sister being there. Okay, so I remember something. She was there. Where is there? What was grandma's that I would've taken, and that Leo would've traded for? Leo doesn't trade for anything unless it's electronic and new. I can't believe I tried to trade him our kitchen chairs that one time. What was I thinking? Mom would've been pissed. But she's pissed now. Why wouldn't he take the chairs? At least those weren't grandma's. I can't believe I sold off something of grandma's to get high. Mom loves her so much. I love mom so much. She's been gone probably about twelve years now. I can't imagine mom being gone. But she's gone now. At least not forever. I'm glad grandma never saw me like this. But she can see me now. She's looking down on me and she's probably upset. Maybe not. Mom said that she was a very forgiving and understanding person. She died in the house. Three days after Christmas. I miss her. Maybe she's keeping mom company now while I'm away. Consoling her.'

"What the fuck!"

As Matthew had sliced open a bag, pieces of human shit flew around the room. Luckily, no one got hit.

"Go get the shop-broom and sweep that shit up."

As Matthew tried to sweep it up, he ended up just smearing and pushing it around. He told Raul he couldn't get it very well and the latter said, "don't worry about it right now. It happens. We'll get it later."

It must have been about ten a.m. It was hot now and there wasn't a wind blowing and so the loading area was stuffy and stinky. A mixture of bodily fluids, along with their own sweat from their soaked bodies hung in the air. Matthew's body started to ache. Each bag must have weighed twenty pounds, and the repetition of working the same few muscles over and over again every time he lifted, and the same few muscles each throwing of contents started to drain him. "Can I get some water," he finally asked.

"Yeah, go ahead but hurry back."

Matthew went to the water fountain at the other end of the loading area but to his amazement it didn't work.

"You gotta go to the bathroom sink inside," yelled Chuy.

Walking inside, Matthew collided with a white man in a suit just a few years older than himself coming out of the restroom.

"Watch it you fucking peon. I oughtta kick you in the fucking face. You got your fucking monkey sweat on my suit."

"It was an accident."

"It was an accident," he mocked. "What are you even doing off the line?"

"Getting some water."

"There's a time for that. It's called your fucking lunch break. I don't think you understand how hard my father works to make sure losers like you have jobs so that you can go on with your pathetic lives."

"I really don't have time for your shit. You spoiled fucking brat. You wanna bitch about it, go bitch about it to him and tell him to fix our fucking water fountain," and he went into the bathroom and drank from the sink. When he left, the guy stood in the hallway and said, "You got some fucking nerve," but Matthew didn't say anything or turn around to look at him. When he got back outside, Raul asked what took so long and Matthew told him about the guy.

"That's Thad, he's basically second in charge here behind his father. What'd you say?"

"I don't know. I bitched him out. I told him to go bitch to his dad and not to me and to fix the fountain. Oh, and I called him a spoiled brat."

"Mad respect fool," said Chuy.

"I can't believe your standing here right now."

"What do you mean?"

"I can't believe he didn't fire you on the spot."

"I think I just caught him off-guard."

"I'm sure you did." I'm really glad you did that. He needed to hear that. I just hope it doesn't cost you your job. None of us have ever stood up to him like that."

"Why? No offense but y'all two look tougher than me."

"It's not about being tough," said Raul. "It's about doing what's right. And what's right is being there for my family. In prison I woulda snapped his fuckin neck like a popsicle stick but I can't do that now cuz I ain't trying to go back there. What are my little boy and girl supposed to do if I go back to prison? What are they supposed to eat? They're worth more to me than my pride. They're worth more to me than my ego. Even if it means taking shit from a prick like Thad. Even if I have to fight off everything within me that says 'yo stomp that bitch.' I'ma do it. Cuz I'ma be there for my kids. You best believe that. And he knows this. He knows I'ma changed man. He knows I ain't the gangbangin hardhead I used to be. And so, he pushes me. But more than anything, he knows that I have no recourse. That we have no recourse. Not just me and Chuy but La Raza. Look, I gotta rap-sheet a mile long. Ain't no other place gonna hire me. Plus, I got my kids. So, he thinks he can shit on me, on us. But I'ma keep my head up and one day karma will kick in."

"So, why do you think he allowed me to do that?"

"Cuz you white fool. Hate to say it but it's true," said Chuy.

"As much as I don't like to jump to race, I think he's right. There's a certain level of shit the white Man has to take from other white folks. And I say man with a capital M cuz I'm not talkin every white person but just those at the top. They have a reasonable level of shit they're expected to take from people like you. But there's absolutely no level of anything people like Thad have to take from people like us. Not if you're brown or black in America."

"He's right fool," said Chuy. "How old are you?"

"I'm eighteen."

"Look, I'm not much older than you. And when I was your age, I got busted writing bad checks. Felony fraud fool. You woulda thought them hoes was made of rubber cuz they bounced back at your boy. I sat up in County for nine months awaiting trial. My mom spent her retirement trying to keep me out of prison. And it worked but we're broke now. And I got six years probation as the plea deal. I can't smoke. I can't drink. I can't do nothin but hey it's cool fool. I'm not in prison. But you know what? I can't get a job nowhere decent now either. And I wasn't even convicted fool. Now what kinda dumb shit is that? Some fucked up shit. What ever happened to innocent until proven guilty? You sayin a felony is so powerful that just the accusation prevents me from getting jobs. That the weight it carries is so forceful that just the act of someone alleging it hangs over me for life. And Thad knows that. He hired me. He saw the glimmer of hope in my eyes when he told me I was hired. But he did it to mistreat me. I honestly believe that. You should see how he treats Ms. Mendoza in there. Always sexually harassing her and shit. Anyway, I have to help support the house with my mom. I have to have a job on probation. No place will hire me. A young Mexican that talk wit a lil slur. I'm seen as a threat to white society. They think I'm comin for their picket fences and shit. So, you know what that means? If I can't get a job. But I have to have a job, or I go to prison. And I ain't goin to prison. Not after what my mom did for me. Not after what it cost her and how much that would hurt her. That means I'm gonna put up with dumb fucks like Thad and their shit."

Matthew had been accepted into the group and the three worked on until lunch. They went to the lunchroom and Matthew sat; he didn't have any food. Chuy noticed and gave him one of the two PB & J sandwiches he had and one of his two apples. Matthew asked if there was anyone that he could bum a smoke from. Chuy said, "I got you fool," and went to an old Hispanic man eating his lunch. Chuy pointed to Matthew, said a few things, and the old man nodded his head approvingly. Without taking his eyes off Matthew, he reached into his pack for one and gave it along with a single match to Chuy. Matthew thanked Chuy and on his way out he thanked the old man in first English and then Spanish. Out of the corner of his eye, he saw Jerry talking with some people in the corner but didn't acknowledge that he had seen him.

Outside on the building's front steps, he sat in the shade and inhaled the fumes savoringly. Matthew commiserated with the hapless Astrodome before him. He heard the door open behind him and dress shoes approach steadily. Thad stood next to where Matthew sat. He lit a cigarette and said, "you're not allowed to smoke here." Matthew wanted to punch him in the throat but remembered what people must endure, and what Raul and Chuy were putting up with for their families. 'I need to do that for mom. Fuck this guy.' And so, Matthew finished his cigarette in the sultry sun out by the street. The blacktop reflected the heat right back at him. He couldn't stop thinking of his mom and how he would do anything, whatever it took, to make up for what he'd done, whatever that was, and earn her trust back. While he braced himself for the second half of the workday, a single tear undulated across his cheek and dripped silently from his lowered chin to the earth below.

V

That afternoon they chatted at intervals while at others they largely remained silent. Matthew was too tired to desire conversation. He tried to solely concentrate on one thing, lifting, cutting, and tossing bags of dirty linens. But his mind wandered. He thought of little outside his mother and what could have happened. Upon cutting a bag open a quarter flew from it. Matthew's eyes followed it through the air and then as it rolled across the cement floor. Click.

Matthew sat drunk on the floor of his mom's closet. Drifting off, his body momentarily swayed back and forth. He placed his hands on the carpet and steadied himself. Underneath a shoe rack sat plastic storage tubs filled with silver coinage. His grandmother and grandfather had owned and operated a tavern in his mother's hometown east of Lansing in the late 50s and early 60s. These coins were from the jukebox in that tavern. Matthew opened the plastic containers. He was primarily interested in quarters and they had to be minted before 1964.

'How much oxy do I need? Look at all this, it's really more like how much oxy do I want? Xanax first though.'

Matthew managed to get in a kneeling position. Reaching to the football shaped toybox from his childhood that his mother kept tucked away in the corner of her closet under hanging clothes, Matthew removed the lid. He reached his arm deep in the toybox and dug around. His mother had kept his and his sister's favorite childhood toys here. Not being able to locate the bottle by touch, he briefly struggled to get to his feet and then looked inside. He quickly moved aside Buzz and Woody, Jibber-Jabber, and his Beanie Babies Snort and Dottie not wanting to stare in the face tangible relics of a more innocent time. He soon found it; the bottle rattled, and he brought it to the surface. Unscrewing the cap, he poured a miniature mountain of alprazolam into his sweaty palm. His body became warm. Marveling at their crisp, green, delicious form for a minute, he took two and returned the bottle to his mother's new hiding place. It had taken him less than twenty-four hours this time to find it, but she was getting more clever. If he could adeptly manage, he'd eat the entire month's supply over the course of a few days before she noticed.

Returning to the quarters, Matthew removed a three-gallon Ziplock bag from his pocket. 'If these are gonna bring me five bucks a piece then eighty should be enough. I need to hurry; Mark L will be here soon.' He heard the front door open. 'Who the fuck is that?' Mom's at work... can it be? His sister's voice called out his name.

Matthew didn't have time to put anything away. A few moments later his sister's shadow darkened the doorway thereby bringing his sin to light. Each was dumbfounded but for different reasons. For a whole minute, he sat, and she stood in silence. The air hung with unendurably bitter tension so thick that it could've been cut with a knife. Finally, she spoke.

"What're you doing?" she asked rhetorically.

"I'm just checking out these coins. I've always wanted to look at them."

"No, you're not. You're stealing them. Those were grandma's."

"I am not!" said Matthew, offended.

"Matthew, you're holding a Ziplock bag."

"Look," Matthew conceded. "I just need a little money. I can cut you in," he implored.

"I gotta go, I can't be part of this. I'm calling mom. I can't believe you."

"No! Don't call mom. Don't go."

But she was already out the front door by the time he got to his feet. Rushing in a hobble to the front door, Matthew saw through the unstained leadlight glass the headlights of her car as it pulled out into the street and accelerated around the curve that the house sat on. He rested his head on his hands which lay on the glass inlay. He sank in incredulity to the wooden floor of the small foyer and then rolled over on to the small rug at its center. 'Mom's gonna know,' he thought in terror. 'She's gonna be upset.' The alprazolam started to first warm his chest and then radiated outward to his extremities. He lay prostrate in physical ecstasy and mental anguish. An indeterminate amount of time passed, and then he heard a car door shut. Mark L had come for the coins.

The partial re-memory of what had happened caused the drudgery of that afternoon to pass even slower. Thoughts of his mother and the fecal fumes worked in tandem to make him dizzy. The heat topped it off to make him sick. Running to the grass outside the loading area, he puked and heaved several times. The sweat dripped from his forehead to join the mush pile. Raul came up behind him and told him to go ahead and go home. Not once had he spoken to either him or Chuy that afternoon about what was torturing him.

He decided not to wait for Jerry. Walking to the train stop he tried to make his thoughts coherent but couldn't. They mushed together into an unidentifiable object like the mass in the grass. On the train he laid back on the plastic seating, closed his eyes, and listened for the audio recording to say 'Ensemble/HCC doors open left.' He shuffled pallidly one block south to 1083. Walking in the door, the two Roberts and Hugh stood at the base of the long wooden staircase trying to coax a man named Alejandro down.

"What's goin on?" he asked.

"He failed his UA and now won't get his stuff and leave," said the older Robert.

"What he fail for?"

"Meth and heroin."

"I just about had enough of this motherfucker," Hugh said, turning to Matthew.

"How long's this been going on for?"

"About forty-five minutes," said the bald-headed younger Robert.

"Now, Alejandro," Hugh spoke. "The reason I ain't call the law on you yet is cuz I like you but I'm fixin to if you don't get the hell outta here this instant. You tryin my patience."

"Puny humans, your weapons against me are futile," said Alejandro. After having said this he leaped out over the staircase. Flight lasted only but a moment. Gravity took effect and he soon bounced, folded, and tumbled down the long, wooden staircase. At the bottom, he lay unconscious for a few seconds. Remarkably, he soon pushed himself up, jumped vigorously to his feet, and ran out the door. The four stared at each other. Hugh broke the silence chuckling, "these crazy motherfuckers." The older Robert, still registering what he had just seen, responded, "yeah, I'll say." Without saying a word, Matthew started to climb the stairs feeling sick and exhausted. "Oh, this came for you today," said Hugh in his raspy voice, reaching into his back pocket. He handed Matthew an envelope. Matthew nodded to gesture appreciation and then slowly mounted the stairs. Getting to his bed, he tore open the envelope. It was written by his mother's hand.

Matthew,
I will always Love you!
You are my son, my first born
+ you are a beautiful child — I
want that child back! I can

hardly see this as the tears flow
down my face + and cloud my eyes.
The love I have for you is forever!
I have no idea how we got
here, I want a nice life.
I had no idea things were as bad
as they truly are. I don't understand
your pill addiction. Or apparently
anything else going on with you.
I feel like we have lived a life of
lies. Why do you do these things?
Then I blame myself, you know
I am trying to maintain the
house + our lives. I really
don't know what to say. The last
2-3 years have been hell at times.
And I feel sick about all of the
horrible things that have happened
to us, + in turn drama we have
brought on ourselves.
Just talked to you. I just
don't understand how you continue
this path.
I do love you!
Mom

Matthew pulled his blanket over his head, rolled to face the wall, and began to silently cry. He sobbed as quietly as he could. The other men in the room thought it best not to disturb him. They'd ask at a later time.

VI

That night Matthew slept soundly and unencumbered. He lay imperturbable to the crawlers which routinely made nocturnal feasts of his hands, swelling both their bodies and his fingers in the process. He received the assurance that he had been desperately aching for and seeking over the almost two weeks he'd been relocated, the knowledge that his mother still loved him. Work went by easier. Matthew punched a timecard, chatted with the guys, and put in an honest day's work.

However, the next Wednesday, exactly a week later, Matthew didn't feel like working. So, he decided not to. But it was payday, so he had to at least go in to pick up his check. Ms. Mendoza chastised him, but he didn't care, he finally had some money. Stepping on a north bound train to head back to the Home, Matthew tore open his check. It was quite a bit less than he expected, $303. It would only cover an additional two-week period and leave him with a little pocket-money. This disheartened him as it meant he would immediately need to find something else. Getting back to the Home, Matthew went to pay some rent.

"Usually," started Hugh searching for the right words. "We like for people to pay they whole month at a time. This is fine. But just for future reference, it's easier for us to keep track of that way. And you don't want nobody screwin wit yo money. Say, why ain't you at work now?"

"I quit. It was just a shitty job," said Matthew uneasily, not wanting to say that he simply didn't feel like going to work that day and therefore sound lazy.

"Shitty? Shitty how? Lots of jobs is shitty. Hell, a lot of times this job is a load of shit. But we put up with them. We don't just quit."

"It was just a toxic work environment."

"Okay, Okay. Well, you been here how many days now… nineteen and today is the… third… and yo rent was paid up until the sixteenth, add two weeks to that which means as of right now April 30th is the last day you paid up fo. But uh, start lookin for work again. And, if that position, I was tellin you about open up, I'll come and talk to you. It might be real soon actually."

"Thanks Hugh."

Stepping outside, Matthew went to talk to Jason who was smoking in the parking lot.

"What's crackin patna?"

"Not much, just gotta find some more work."

"Shit, me too. We in da same boat. Matter fact that's why I'm posted up outchea. The temp agency ain't workin out and they said this woman that be by every so often needin guys to do shit was here earlier and said she'd be back. So, I don't wanna miss that. Even if it's only for a day. I need the bread."

"Oh, okay. Mind if I wait with you?"

"Be my guest. If it was someone else, I might have an issue cuz some of dese folks don't know how to act, and I don't want them messin up dis opportunity. But you cool. You young and jus be doin yo thing, ain't bother nobody, ain't loud, got manners and all dat. You really just be tryin to get back to yo mom's and I respect that."

"preciate it. Hey, you got an extra smoke?"

"Yeah, I gotcha," said Jason, handing him one.

Matthew took it and suggested they go to the Serenity Garden. "We can keep an eye on the parking lot from there." They sat at a table smoking under the trees with the wind blowing the late morning clouds aimlessly overhead. Matthew wondered what type of clouds they were. 'I can't remember any of those names from school.' The clandestine corner of natural scenery afforded Matthew an ephemeral escape from financial worry. Flowing with the breeze, the Spanish moss hung low and stretched out. A male cardinal landed in the grass a short distance from where they sat and quickly yet quietly pecked up a grasshopper who just moments before was on a quest to obtain its own morning meal. Although just a short walk from the city's epicenter, this teeny, forested rectangle inexplicably kept all commotion at bay. It seemed impregnable.

A minute later, a tan minivan rolled into the gravel lot throwing up white dust and dirt with its entry.

"You want to make some money helping me around the house?" yelled an older white woman from its window.

"Bet," said Jason to Matthew and the two got up and headed toward the van. The juxtaposition of the two coming her way struck her as intense. Upon reaching the vehicle she said, "I think I'll just be needing his help," indicating Matthew.

"Are you sure? I can do whatever you need me to do? said Jason.

"Yeah, I'm afraid I'm sure. Thanks though."

Feeling an underlying tension, Jason walked off, shook his head and mumbled "ain't that bout a bitch." When he was at a safe distance, she continued, "Do you have any friends that could help out?"

"Just him," said Matthew.

"No, I mean friends more like yourself. You never can be too careful."

"You mean young?" said Matthew in an attempt to further ferret out her prejudice.

"Not necessarily, just more our type."

"No, it's just me," said Matthew angered.

"Okay, well then get in."

"I'm Martha," she said in a nasally voice.

"I'm Matthew."

Martha pulled out and headed north. She began to describe the menial tasks that she wanted completed, scrubbing floors, tubs, sinks, and baseboards. She sounded a bit off her rocker and Matthew grew anxious. 'What have I gotten myself into? I hope this goes okay and I can make a little money. She doesn't seem quite right though. That sucks for Jason. Stupid bitch. Unless he dodged a bullet. Only if this lady's nuts. I guess I'll see.'

About ten minutes later, they pulled up to a townhouse. Before getting out of the van she said, "you have to take your shoes off at the door." Inside, cleaning products in mass quantities lay stacked around the living room's perimeter. Two litter boxes sat visibly over capacity with piles of cat shit starting to accumulate outside of them.

"You have to wash your hands before you touch anything," she said annoyingly. "You have to use more soap than that. God, what do they teach you at that home anyway? You're not one of those druggies are you kid? Wait, no, don't answer that. I probably won't like your response. You look like one. You know, it wouldn't kill you to take some pride in your appearance. You're not going to find yourself a nice little girlfriend dressing like that. I hope you're not a homosexual either because this is a house of god. Anyway, you look like a thug with those shorts and the burnholes all down the front of them. Didn't your mother raise you better than that?"

"Don't you have something for me to do?" Matthew interjected.

He had been gridding his teeth, thinking "I'm doing this to get back to mom. I'm doing this to get back to mom. I'm doing this to get back to..." but the questioning of his mother's parental abilities excited a defensive mechanism that knew no filter.

"Are you really going to be that rude this entire time because if so, you can leave. I don't need a hoodlum in my house telling me what to do."

Matthew was deliberate with his breathing throughout the tirade. Upstairs, she had Matthew fill a bucket with hot soapy water while she sat perched up on her filthy bed. Her bedroom and bathroom were in a state of total disarray. Scum thicker than that at the Home caked her tub and tile floor yet cleaning products were everywhere. Christian paraphernalia hung on every wall. The bathroom countertop lay strewn with half-full bottles of tranquilizers and painkillers. At the sight of them, Matthew grew flush. He wanted to sneak some. But her bed was a panoptic vantage point from where she could sit judgingly and through the reflection of the bathroom mirror oversee all his tedious scrubbings and other various toils. She had several wine bottles on her nightstand. Periodically, Matthew would hear the glugging of her filling a glass while he worked. For two hours, he labored tirelessly while she sat captiously and capriciously barking directives. The only reason that Matthew held out for as long as he did was due to the belief that she might leave him unattended, even for just a moment. His pharmaceutical sleight of hand was unmatched, and he held stubbornly to the hope that he would get an opportunity to put it into action.

The opportunity finally presented itself. As she rose to retrieve something from her closet, Matthew deftly yet unscrupulously poured quantities from the two bottles that he had already designated as his top two choices, careful to leave a few in each as a lame attempt to cover the crime. Having finally secured a hefty supply, Matthew threw up his hands. Without saying anything, he made his way to the stairs.

"Where do you think you're going?" her voice rang out piercingly.

"I can't take your shit any longer. You want someone to clean your house, fine. But you're not gonna talk to me the way you have anymore."

"My god, what was it that I said?"

"It's everything you've said. You're crazy. I can't take it anymore."

Matthew left through the front door, put on his shoes, and made his way in the direction that he thought the Home was. The pills clattered joyfully in his pocket as his gait lightly bounced them up and down. He caressed them, feeling the two distinct shapes as he turned them over between his fingers. Matthew was both uneasy and uncertain of his next move. 'If I break these in half, this should last me a long time. What if I get caught? I'll get kicked out and mom won't take me back. That's why I can only take half of one at a time. I can do that. I can discipline myself. I have to or else I won't get to go back home. What if they know that I'm fucked up? They won't know because I won't be fucked up because I'll make sure to only take halves. What if I took a handful? No, I won't do that. I can't do that or else, no mom," but just the thought elicited a single undesired and unprompted rock in his step. Splitting one in half while walking down a residential side street, Matthew dry mouthed it on an empty stomach. He immediately grew warm. He was brimming with satisfaction. 'I got these. Mom still loves me. Everything is starting to pan out okay. I knew that if I just kept doing the next right thing that God would look out for me.'

VII

Returning to the Home just before two o'clock, Matthew bumped into George outside the meeting hall. "Say old boy, you tryna get one of your meetings in?" "Sure," said Matthew knowing that he had an hour to kill before he could put his stash away and not wanting to appear too eager to dodge a meeting. They took their seats and chatted, a few minutes later the meeting began with a man first discussing meeting mechanics and then inducing the group to join in prayer.

Matthew felt warm and somewhat weightless. A feeling he yearned to obtain ever since he mysteriously appeared at the Home steadily crept to the forefront of his being. All the meetings at the Home's meeting hall were open to the public, many were facilitated by outsiders, and as Matthew looked around the room, he only recognized a few faces. The coveted sensations that the half a pill aroused in him were stronger than anticipated, and as the first person spoke, his eyes grew heavy as he resisted a yawn to prevent torpidity from taking hold.

A woman spoke, "I had to get in here, and get to a meeting today. I was starting to feel all sorts of ways. It's cunning, and I just know that ain't no good for me. It creeps up on ya too. One minute I feel fine but before I know it, I feel all throwed off. And that's how I started to feel today. And I know God wanted me to get a meeting today too cuz he had me get off early. So, I brought myself here and this where I'm gon sit and hear me some solution. That's all I got to say, thank y'all."

Thank yous came in unanimity.

"Alright, that's a good start. Who's next?"

"I'll go," said the man in front of Matthew leaning forward as he started to speak. "I like what this woman here had to say. Cuz she recognized it and took action. And that's harder to do then it sounds. Cuz I be so sick that I don't be realizin that I'm sick. And for the newcomers when I say 'sick' I mean spiritually sick. Not the flu. It's that sickness that insists on me making every relationship in my life dysfunctional. And worst of all, it be tellin my ass that I ain't sick. What other sickness causes the sufferer to not just think but believe they ain't sick? Maybe dementia or Alzheimer's or something like that but other than that that's it. So, to make sure I don't start to get too sideways, I come to these here meetings and listen. You gotta remain teachable. Cuz as soon as I start to believe that I know it all, I'll start to convince myself that I don't need these meetings. That I don't need to call my sponsor and that I don't need nobody's help. So, one of the many ways that I try to keep myself from getting too sick, is to be in a meeting everyday cuz you can't fall off the middle of the roof. I'ma shut up now. Thank y'all for listinin.

A multitude of *thank yous* poured in. And Matthew briefly thought of Alex.

"Alright that was another good one. How bout another?"

"I'll go," said George sitting up straight. "What I know is that when I start to feel that way, it ain't gon take not but a minute for me to go back out, if I don't take action right then. If I take action, I can do something about it. But I also know how it's gonna go if I let that sickness take hold. Cuz I done this before. This ain't my first rodeo. It'll start off with me probably convincing myself that I don't need a meeting or maybe even that I'm not an alcoholic and a dope fiend. That maybe I overreacted. And don't get me wrong now, I'll still be aware of all my consequences, don't get it twisted. That's why I'm gonna be so damn careful this next time. Nobody think they more careful than an alcoholic bout to relapse. Don't get me fooled. Sometimes I don't even know that I'm bout to relapse. I'll just be mindin my own business, goin bout my lil way when bam the opportunity presents itself. And you see, it's not that I be planning to use. I don't just be planning to wreck my shit. It's not like I'd wake up that morning and think 'you know what? I think I'd like to destroy my life today.' No, we all know it don't be like that. But if I don't do the work, when the occasion arises, I find that I then don't have a spiritual defense to sidestep it. And because I've burned myself so many times before, because I remember what the poison did to me the last time, I'll devise a plan ha ha. I can mastermind some shit. I be like the villain in a James Bond movie but instead of blowin up the world, it be my own life. And it's funny, well not really, cuz I be the only person who can't see that. I be the only person that don't see that B comes after A. Once I devise a plan, I start thinkin 'well you never know, if I do it like this it could be C.' So, after I come up with my stupid little plan, whatever it may be, only drinkin half the liquor, only doin half the eight-ball; I'm only gonna shoot half the dope, I'll finally do it. You ever notice how we alcoholics really like things in twos. You ask an alcoholic how much they have to drink, and I guarendamntee ya he'll say 'two' or 'just a couple.' Now, that's when we already been out a minute. But when we first go back out everything's in halves. And what are halves but two of one, the whole. Anyway, so I put that poison in my body whether I was planning to or not, that's just what we do, and sometimes outta fear, I'll follow my little plan for a little while. Fear can do that to ya. Fear can do amazin things. I'm driven by fear, you're driven by fear, we are a species driven by fear. Fear of endin up like I once was can often keep me relatively under the radar, relatively in control for some time. But that control is a delusion. Cuz as soon as that fear starts to go away, my little plan becomes less and less important to follow. That was the whole reason for the plan in the first place, to avoid or defer some sort of consequence I fear from happenin. My willingness and ability to follow my delusional little plan, if you can even call it them two things, is tied to the amount of pain that I'm currently in. Cuz fear causes pain. I don' like to be scared cuz that makes me uneasy; it makes me uncomfortable. You ever wonder how us drug addicts be getting out of prison and stayin sober for lengths of time without takin any spiritual action? The answer's fear. Fear of goin back to prison, fear of arrest, fear of losin ya job, fear of divorce, fear of being kicked out the house, fear of losin a loved one, can either keep us sober or outwardly managing our addictions for remarkably long periods of time. But as soon as that element of fear leave, so does my control. And I'll be not just as bad as I was before I put that substance back in my body, but I'll be even worse. If we're not actively tryin to better ourselves spiritually, it's just a matter of time before we either go back out or twist off for good. And I don't want that to happen to me. And that's why I'm here. Thank y'all for listening."

Thank yous came from everybody.

"How about that young man sittin right next to you? Yeah, you. Would you like to share?"

"I guess. I'm Matthew and I'm pretty new around here. Been here… going on three weeks. And I've tried to get sober before. I had been working with my sponsor for a couple months before I got here. I wasn't sober the whole time though. I'd get a few days or a few weeks and then go back out. But like George said I thought I could control it. Until one day, I did some stupid shit. I stole some of my mom's stuff. I'm honestly not really sure what happened. But I really upset her, and she doesn't want me home for a while. And so, I'm here. I'm just gonna try to learn while I'm here. I know that I can't go on like I was. That something's gotta give. But I'm just not sure what. I'm really just in the process of trying to earn my mom's trust back. I don't know how long it'll take but I'll be here in the meantime just trying to learn from y'all and trying to do what's right. God knows that I love my mom and that I'd do anything for her. So, I'm just gonna prove it to her instead of just tellin her that I love her. Because she's heard all that before, but she wants to see it. That's it."

Matthew's warm and fuzzy body was in full effect. But it didn't stop him from wondering what everybody had thought of what he had to say. He was scared people were judging him. He was scared that he had sounded dumb. But most of all, he was scared that people could see right through him. That they knew that he was a liar and a thief. Not out in addiction but in the meeting hall. That they knew he wasn't serious and that he had just lied to all their faces by feeding them a load of crap. He was most scared that they knew what he had just done. That they could read the usage right on his face and that they would expose him for who he truly was, a phony. That they were going to tell on him and get him kicked out and then he'd be out on the street and that he'd never see his mom again and that she'd hate him.

Between the fear and the mild sedation, it was hard for Matthew to pay attention during the rest of the meeting. Fears and thoughts, both separate and intermixed, swirled agonizingly free in his head. By the time the meeting came to a close, he had managed to quell his anxiety. 'I'll just take these. These are it. And only in halves. After that I'm done. Done. I'll find another job and just wait until I can go back home and see mom.' As Matthew held George and another man's hand during the wrap up prayer, he thanked God while he felt the furtive bundle of pills pressed neatly up against his leg.

VIII

A couple weeks later, it was Matthew's nineteenth birthday. He rose slow, lethargic from the whole pill he had taken the night before. He hadn't found another job in the last few weeks nor had he done much looking. The last seventeen days had been a blur. For the first week after he stole the pills, he managed to take just a half a pill at a time. Matthew would rise early with everyone else, shower, go out as if he was looking for work but as soon as he hit the street, he'd take his half. Afterwards, he would roam the city streets aimlessly, frequenting park benches and seedy areas. About an hour before bed, during tv time, he would slip upstairs to his dresser to retrieve another half from inside a sock at its back. Then after that first week, he began incorporating a third half during his wanderings as a sort of midday snack since he wasn't returning to the Home during the day for lunch. The last two days he had taken a full one in the morning and another full one at night. His supply was dwindling at an increasingly rapid rate but that isn't what disturbed him. What bothered him was his obvious inability to stick to a prescribed quota. At this rate, he would be drug tested soon. Remarkably, he had not been popped with a random UA yet, but if he continued to up his dose getting popped wouldn't be random. He couldn't believe that nobody that he knew of suspected anything. Maybe his youth aided in masking the symptoms. Maybe not. All he knew was that getting caught would prolong his suffering, and perhaps make it eternal if he for some reason or another was unable to see his mother again. So, he decided to rid himself of these demons and once again start anew.

Two things that Matthew had done over the course of the last few weeks was get a tracfone and a library card. He hoped to be able to talk to his mother today and was excited at the thought of her wishing him a happy birthday. *Catcher in the Rye* was also almost due back, and so Matthew had a small list of things to accomplish.

At breakfast that morning, Tim ran in the dining hall and said, "Y'all the cops are here." Being Tim, nobody stirred at first, but someone eventually asked why. "I don't know," he responded, "but they're here." Matthew, along with everyone else, scarfed down what food they had left. The pack moved fluidly to the front desk where out the front windows they saw two HPD cars. Duke said, "Y'all can't stand in here. Go on bout y'all's business."

"What's goin on? Someone called from the back.

"Y'all'll find out soon enough. Move around." The pack without a head seamlessly moved out through the kitchen to the courtyard area out back. They saw Hugh move with two HPD behind him. He didn't answer a single inquiry but instead rasped, "Y'all finna see."

The white officer hocked a loogie at the feet of Lester, Jason, and Jerry who were standing off to the side in their own group. A series of exclamations were uttered from the three. The offender, baton in hand, stepped up.

"Y'all are lucky I don't split y'all's stupid fucking skulls," he said trying too hard to sound dangerous. The three were mute. Hugh, who had witnessed the whole incident, addressed the residents saying, "Dammit, would y'all stop making trouble. Can't you see I gotta enough to deal with." The three nodded, anxious to both get the officer off their necks, and to find out why they were here in the first place. Approaching the residential backdoor of the meeting hall and coffee-bar building, the police drew their guns.

"Would y'all put those things away. He's not dangerous," rasped Hugh exasperated.

"We need these for our protection. Don't tell us how to do our jobs unless you want to end up face down on the ground," said the white officer.

"But I'm the one who called y'all. Why you threatening me? Look, I got fifteen to twenty guys who live back here. I can't have y'all pointin pistols in all my residents' faces."

"Where's his bed," asked the black officer robotically.

"When you go upstairs," began Hugh, visibly alarmed. "to the left there's about a dozen beds. It ain't none of them. When you go up the stairs, it's the door to the right. It's the only single bedroom up there. It's right next to the bathroom. You can't miss it."

"It's Daniel," murmured throughout the crowd. Daniel was the head manager, Hugh's boss. "I wonder what he did," echoed through the crowd.

"Before we go in, I'm gonna need you to describe the suspect," stated the white officer.

"He's about six foot two, skinny, middle aged, with shoulder length hair," said Hugh.

"Race?" asked the black officer.

"He white."

Both officers synchronously holstered their firearms, arming themselves instead with batons.

They went in. A few minutes later, Daniel stepped out the backdoor into the alley connected to the courtyard with an officer behind him on each side holding one of his arms. He looked down at first, avoiding the thirty or so faces in the morning sun. Realizing the charade was up, his face oozed despondency when he then looked out at the faces that stared silently back.

"What'd you do?" yelled Tim.

"I didn't do anything," he responded, expecting nothing to come from it.

"Nothin!" exclaimed Hugh. "You've been stealin from the Home long enough. But I finally caught you. I got you on camera. That's right. I put a little camera in the office last night befo I closed up. I seent you."

"Say what you want, I didn't do anything," Daniel hopelessly retorted.

Hugh was livid. "Now you gon lie to my face. First you pass me up for promotion, I don't even want to say why. Then I confront you about missin money a while back and you wanna, you wanna… act like you don't know nothin. When I knew. I knew this whole damn time. I just can't believe it took me this long to figure out how to catch you. Please officers, take this man away from here befo he starts spoutin off some mo bullshit." The officers forcibly placed Daniel in a patrol car. Matthew looked at the lone, low-hung, face in the car and felt sorry for it. He knew what it was like to make mistakes, especially in sobriety. The crowd dispersed a few minutes later when the car drove into downtown.

Book in hand, pill sock in pocket, Matthew set out for the library. He made his way north along Main Street to the light-rail station following the invisible trail of the police car. At the station, two metro cops asked a black man sitting on a bench to produce either his ticket or proof of purchase. Not wanting to pay the fare, Matthew approached a kiosk and tapped his driver's license pretending it was a Q card. A moment later, Matthew sat on an empty bench to pass the time until the next train came. It was a Saturday, and so his mother wouldn't be at work. It was now just after nine, and he decided to give her a call. Since arriving at the Home, Matthew had only spoken to his mother twice over the phone. She wasn't either yet able to communicate her thoughts and feelings very well on the phone since his departure or she was unwilling to. So, the conversations had been very brief. Dialing the number, it began to ring.

"Hello," his mother's voice said wearily.

"Hi mom, how are you? I love you."

"I love you too. Happy birthday sweetheart."

"Thank you, mom. I miss you."

"I miss you too, but you know you can't come home."

"I know but soon?"

"Honestly Matthew, probably not."

"Okay, I figured," said Matthew sadly. "I had to ask."

"You know you have to get better first."

"I know."

"So, what are you going to do today?"

"I'm on my way to the library to return a book."

"What book?"

"*Catcher in the Rye.*"

"Oh, I read that a long time ago." There was an uncanny irony in her voice at the mention of the title.

"Well happy birthday again sweetheart. I'm gonna make some breakfast. But I hope you have a good day today. I love you."

"I love you too mom. I'll talk to you later. Bye."

"Bye, honey," and she hung up.

Matthew could see the train approaching from the south. Love for his mother swelled in his heart alongside disappointment at not being able to see her. Trying to compose himself, he stepped onto the train. Looking westward out the window, he watched the light flickerings of an oblique morning sun flash intermittently between buildings from behind him. 'I'm gonna get better for mom. I gotta get rid of these things. They're killing me. They're gonna kill me. They're killing mom. They're gonna kill mom. What if mom died? What if mom died because of me? Can people actually die from a broken heart? I don't want to find out. *I want a nice life. I don't understand my addiction. I don't understand anything else going on with me either. I feel like I have lived a life of lies. Why do I do these things? It's my fault. I try to maintain. Hell at times. I feel sick. Drama. I do love you.*'

Getting off at Main Street Square, Matthew headed west on McKinney. Looking at the pavement as he shuffled along, he wondered where he could ditch his stash unseen. Shifting his gaze up, Matthew edged his way down the busy sidewalk staring at the gleaming brilliance of Wells Fargo Plaza. 'A trashcan? No, too obvious.' A police horse trotted by. 'What if cops used horses to sniff out drugs? I'd be fucked.' Light now bounced off the Plaza. Redirecting his eyes to the ground, Matthew fixed his view on a sleeping homeless man that lay huddled up against a building. 'He'd like these. Charitable. No, better not.' The library lay erudite ahead. Homeless dominated its grounds out front. Crossing the street, Matthew saw his opportunity. Just before he reached the opposite sidewalk, he pretended to tie his shoe. Stealthily retrieving the sock from his pocket, he emptied its contents in a storm sewer. "So long," he whispered to the descending tablets.

Walking up the pathway, Matthew turned back to stare amazed at the Plaza once more now that the sun no longer impeded his appreciation. A second later, he bumped into a man standing on the sidewalk.

"Hey man, you needa be more careful," said the questionably homeless man.

"I'm sorry, I wasn't paying attention."

"You ain't from around here, are ya?"

"No, I'm from Houston. Why?"

"You starin up at them buildings like you a tourist. Like you ain't seen nothin like em befo."

"I just got a lot on my mind, sorry."

"That's alright, if you tryna relax, I can hook you up with a kush joint fo five dollas."

"Fake bake?"

"Mm-hmm."

"No, I don't want any of that."

"Well can you help me out wit just a few dollas. I need to get to San Antonio."

"I wish I could, But I don't have anything." Matthew rubbed his last ten between his fingers in his pocket. "Just here to return a book," he said, moving along.

"Stay in school," the man hollered with a laugh from behind him.

Inside, Matthew checked his return in. He then browsed the section in which he had found it. A massive book caught his eye. The title intrigued him. *Of Human Bondage.* 'Is this BDSM? I hope not.' Reading the back, he decided to go with it. On his way downstairs, the thought of so much physical knowledge compiled in one place briefly overwhelmed him. "This is due back in three weeks on May 11th." "Okay, thank you," said Matthew then heading out. Outside, the radiant sun now shone high overhead.

Matthew headed back to Main Street Square. This time east down Lamar Street. He sauntered along wondering how to spend the rest of his birthday. A couple of businessmen stood in the middle of the sidewalk.

"They caught the second bomber last night. You see that?"

"Yeah, everyone knows that. Fuckin Arab."

"What's the matter with you? He's not even Arab."

"Yeah, well he's Muslim. Is that politically correct enough for you?"

'What are they talking about?' Matthew sat on a nearby bench and lit a cigarette to eavesdrop.

"What does that have to do with anything?"

"You're joking right? They come over here from the dunes of whatever Stan to kill Americans, white Americans, white Christian Americans at that."

"What the fuck are you even talking about? I asked what does him being Muslim have to do with it."

"Are you serious? It has everything to do with it. 9/11. It's Arab terrorists again and again."

"But they're not Arab. They're from Chechnya or wherever in the Caucasus. Which makes them...at least white passing.

You saw their pictures, right? And what do you mean it's Islamic terrorists again and again? What about Atlanta? What about Oklahoma City? The Unabomber, the D.C. sniper, the UT sniper. Huh? What does all that mean to you?"

"Those are old cases. I'm tellin you, it's different now."

"And I'm tellin you we don't know enough at this point to point to religion as a motive. And even if it was, that doesn't reflect all Muslims."

"Say what you want, I'm a patriot. I voted for Cruz. Who did you vote for?"

"Sadler, does that make me any less American? No."

"You wouldn't get it. You weren't in Desert Storm."

"We weren't even talking about any of that. We were talking about Boston. I just can't believe how young the second bomber is. What is he eighteen?"

"Nineteen."

"God, I mean that's almost my son's age. It's like that kid right there," he pointed to Matthew. "blowin some shit up and killin a bunch of people. I can't imagine my son or any kid like that," again indicating Matthew. "doin something like that."

Matthew didn't like being singled out for their discussion and got up to move along. They continued talking. The second man called out to him, "Hey kid, you wouldn't attack America, would you now?"

"No," said Matthew, offended and confused.

He turned his back to them and again headed away. From behind him he heard, "See! I told you. Kids like your son and that kid wouldn't hurt America. You know why? Cuz they're god-fearing, white Americans. As for foreigners, you can't be too sure."

"Bullshit, it has nothin to do with being foreign. People are people. And if those kids in Boston were radicalized that doesn't discount what radicalized Christians do in this country."

Reaching the rail-line, Matthew tapped his driver's license to the kiosk to feign payment. A southbound train had just departed, and the station was empty. Being a weekend, the streets weren't as crowded. He took a seat and processed the conversation he had just overheard. A few minutes later, a man, presumably homeless due to the tatters he wore, walked past Matthew and said, "Motherfucker takin up the whole bench." Matthew stood up angry.

"What are you talking about? There's like five other benches."

"Yeah, but I want that one."

"Well, too bad. I'm sittin here."

"Oh, so you think you own the place."

He reached down and picked up Matthew's book.

"*Of Human Bondage*? What kinda gay shit is this?"

Before Matthew could even ask for it back, the man threw it down on the rail-line.

"What the fuck is your problem? You piece of shit."

"Fuck you," and he pushed Matthew off the platform ledge. He fell about three feet and landed on his side on the tracks next to his book. The man walked off laughing drunkenly. Some people going about their day looked but didn't do anything. Matthew clambered back onto the station platform. Though his leg was scraped, his pride smarted more than anything.

Until the train came, and on the short ride back to Midtown, Matthew's ego worked diligently at its irrational means of self-preservation. 'If I woulda had a gun, I woulda killed that motherfucker. Dead. Splat. End his shit. But then what? I would go to prison and I wouldn't see mom again. Oh, mom. I love you. I'm sorry. That motherfucker had it coming though. I'm not the one. I can't do this. I don't think I can do this. I wonder how far down that drain those pills are? Too far. I can't get them. I'm done with that anyway. For mom, I'm done. New leaf. What if they test me? How long do those even stay in your system? I should start running. I could stand to lose a few pounds anyway. What was that guy's problem? Didn't he know who he was talking to? Doesn't he know who I am? More like was, I've changed. Doesn't he know what I would've done to him in the past? Who I once was? Who I think I am? No, who I once thought I was. That me, gone. The pills, gone. Mom, gone. But if that me returns, if those pills and the liquor comes back then this me gone. No mom, forever. It's just temporary distance, in betweenness, separation, me here and mom elsewhere. I'll earn her trust back. I'll prove it to her. I'll show my father, everybody, the world. Oh god, but I'm not in control. I don't even know when I can go home. I'm powerless. I can't control anything in my life. I'm miserable. If you would have asked me ten years ago, how I thought I'd be now, it wouldn't be like this. No one loves me. Mom loves me. That's everything and everyone who matters but it feels like no one at the same time. I have no one. I hate my life. I hate myself. I'm a loser. Dad's right. I am a loser. But no, I'll show him. I'm gonna do something. But what? Well, I have to stay sober. No good can come from what I've been doing. I can't believe I haven't been caught. I'd be even more miserable then. How did I get here? How did I end up like this? What did I do after I decided to steal the coins? Oh mom, I'm sorry. I'm so sorry. I can't do anything right.'

Getting off at his stop, Matthew wanted to walk and clear his head. He could've gone to the Home because it was a Saturday, but he wasn't ready. Matthew passed the Home walking east along Alabama. Looking to his right, he saw a young white woman sitting on a step outside of a gas station. 'I wonder if she'd… She looks like she might. I'm gonna see.' His heart raced and he felt warm. He felt the way he did when he was about to drink or get high. 'I shouldn't but what if… won't hurt to see.' He started to shake at the thought. His heart pounded vigorously. He knew that he shouldn't but was physically unable to stop himself. He was totally entranced at the thought of hedonic pleasure.

"Hey."

"Hey," she said.

"You tryna make some money?"

"Doin what?"

"Havin fun."

"What? You want some head?"

"Yeah, how much?"

"Ten bucks?" she said, shrugging her shoulders.

"Sure. Where though?"

"You don't have a car, do you?"

"No."

"Okay, that's fine. I know a spot."

She stood up and started walking, dragging her left leg behind her. She wasn't as young as Matthew had first thought, but probably still in her mid to late thirties. She was very skinny and wore jeans and a spaghetti strap tank top. With each step, her sideways foot scraped the sidewalk. It made Matthew uncomfortable how slow they made their way. The Home was just a few blocks away and he dreaded the thought of someone he knew seeing them. Slowing his pace, to walk alongside her, he looked at her face while she determinedly looked ahead. She looked sad, exhausted and inconsolably sad. Matthew thought he may have found the only person in the vicinity more miserable than he. His thoughts caused his heart to pound and his penis to pulsate. 'I'm in control. Someone has to do what I say.'

Just two blocks later, they turned south off Alabama onto Caroline. Matthew was relieved. A few buildings down she said, "here," and turned into a narrow sodden gap hidden behind an overgrown bush poking through fences that separated properties. Matthew had to pull back growth to get to a narrow open slit between the two fences for them to stand. Reaching the muddy, shaded spot, it was more open than he expected. It was broad daylight, and Matthew was just a few yards from the sidewalk but was mostly concealed by herbage. He felt high, woefully high. She knelt, and he pulled down his worn basketball shorts. She sat at eye level for a moment with his untumid and shriveled penis. And though it stirred and internally throbbed, no blood flowed into it. It is as if it didn't want to participate either. But because Matthew was in control, for once, both she and it had to. He held the book clasped against his side. She placed her warm, wet mouth around his short, shy quasi manhood, totally enveloping it. 'I'm in charge.' One, two, three seconds later his tingling yet completely flaccid penis ejaculated intensely into her mouth. She looked up haggardly.

"Wow, that was fast."

"Keep going."

She continued at Matthew's vain command to try to straighten a wet noodle. A minute later, both euphoric and ashamed, he told her she could stop.

"Easiest ten dollars I ever made."

"Yeah, I bet," said Matthew, discontented.

Walking in 1083, Lester stood there and smiled suspiciously.

"I seen you with that girl."

Matthew became flush with horrific embarrassment.

"What?" he stuttered. "I don't know what you're talking about."

"Yeah, okay," said Lester facetiously. "It's okay, I seen Jerry with her the otha day," he continued.

"No, really. I don't know what you're talking about," Matthew inflexibly maintained.

"Alright then playa. You must have a twin. Either that or there's just a whole bunch of young, white cats like you runnin around here," he said sarcastically.

"Yeah, probably someone else."

Lester looked at Matthew sideways and unbelieving but playful.

The older house manager Robert came down the long wooden staircase, eyeing Matthew which made him even more nervous.

"Hugh wants you over at the office," he said addressing Matthew.

"Me? What about?" he responded alarmed.

"I don't know. But he was here maybe a half hour ago. I'd go see him."

"Okay, thanks," said Matthew trying to overcome the worry

rising within him.

Walking through the courtyard, Matthew pondered. 'Why does Hugh want me? What if he saw too? What if Lester told? What if he's gonna test me? Wait, what if she had something? Maybe it's to ask me when I'm gonna have a job. My rent runs out in ten days. Oh god, that was fast. I need to ask for more time. Do they even do that? Maybe not ask but just hint at it. Put it out there. Am I about to be tested? Oh no, I'm gonna be on the street. It doesn't matter how much he likes me, he's gonna have to toss me out. Oh god, Oh mom. She's gonna be so mad. I'm gonna be homeless. Wait, what if I'm not gonna be tested? I don't see how it could be anything but that. I've been walking around here mildly high for weeks. He knows. He's gotta know. Then why's he gonna test me? To make a fool out of me. Punish me. But what if, no, what if he saw? God, I hope not. What would happen? Would I be out on the street? Again, no mom, no home, no nothing. Would he care? Of course. He can't have guys running around here doing stuff like that. What I just did. I don't think Lester told. He wouldn't do that. But what if? No. What if mom found out about…? What if she had…? Something. What? Anything. The big one. How would I know? What if Jerry gave her something, or she gave it to us both. What if I already had something and I just gave her a mouthful of it? No, I don't think so. Probably not. Could count on one hand the girls. Still possible though. But her. Probably couldn't count on a couple dozen hands. It was only a second. Does that make a difference? I hope so. What was with that? I felt high. Maybe because it's been a while. No, there was something different. She had to. Well didn't have to but needed to. Necessitous. Transactional. Bondage. I say she do. I wonder if she had a Maurice. Mom, I'm sorry. I'm getting better. I promise.'

Walking in Hugh's office, Matthew held his teeth from chattering. Hugh sat writing with a cigarette in his mouth. He gazed up at Matthew, puffed some smoke, and just stared stonily for a few moments without saying anything.

"You want a job?" he finally asked.

"Yes… I do… sir," said Matthew unprepared.

"Good." He paused for a moment. "You there this morning?"

"Yes, I saw it."

"Well, that's why I thought a spot might be opening up, but I just didn't know when. I had to catch the son of a bitch. I knew I would. I just didn't know when though."

"I see," responded Matthew, unsure as to how he should follow up. "So, what're you gonna have me do?" he managed after a moment's hesitation.

"Well, I thought originally I'd have you at front desk and move Duke over to coffee-bar, but he don't wanna do that. So, four days a week you gon be at coffee-bar. Monday, Tuesday, Thursday, Friday. Monday, Tuesday mornings you'll do coffee-bar and then Thursday, Friday evenings. Now Wednesday afternoons you'll be front desk. It's easy, piece of cake."

"How much will I get paid?"

"You ain't gon be makin shit." Matthew chuckled but Hugh wasn't joking. "You gon be putting in forty hours a week. Five eight-hour shifts. You get paid every two weeks eighty-nine dollas. That comes out to about a dolla twelve an hour. But yo rent is now taken care of, you still get three hot meals a day, and at the coffee-bar you make tips. Hell, you probably make more there than you do on the payroll."

"Cool, alright. The only reason I asked was because I wanted to know if I'd have cigarette money."

"Yep, that's about all you gon have. All you'll be able to afford. But that's good. Nothin good ever come from a man havin too much money." Matthew nodded. Hugh continued, "It comes with a few other little perks too. You ain't gonna be drug tested no mo. Ain't gotta worry about randoms. Well not worry, only worry if you doin somethin that you know you ain't supposed to be doin. So, now you just ain't gotta deal with em. Only time you gon be tested is if you fuckin up, you know, actin suspicious. You also gotta good work week, Monday through Friday. Most the other staff ain't got that. So, you can leave if you want Friday night. Go back home or whatever for the weekend. Just as long as you back at the coffee-bar six a.m. Monday mornin to open it up. Other thing, you movin out of 1083 and goin back behind the coffee-bar. You ain't gon be upstairs in the attic with the residents. You staff now. You gon have the downstairs room next to me."

"I get my own room?" Matthew asked excitedly.

"Hell naw you don't get yo own room," Hugh rasped. "Only people that get they own room is Daniel and me. Well not no mo. It's gon be me and uh… me and uh Robert now who got they own rooms. The little old Robert. Well older Robert. He prolly my age. I better watch who I be callin old. Anyway, I'm promotin him to assistant manager." A groan from Duke was heard out in the hallway.

"So, who's gonna be the other house manager now?"

"That don't matter to you. After today you ain't gon be livin there no mo. But hell if I know. I'm gonna let Robert figure that out. Young Robert that is."

"So, who am I gonna be rooming with?"

"Billy and Willy. You know them, don't you?"

"Billy's the real big white guy with the real long combed back hair that always looks wet, right?"

"Yeah, that's him. He runs the computer lab in the back of the coffee-bar. I don't know why though. I never see nobody use it. You ever been back in it?"

"No."

"That's what I thought."

"So, who's Willy? I don't know a Willy on staff."

"Willy not on staff anymore. But he used to damn near run this place. Used to have my job. Had it when I showed up here, what was it… eight years ago. He ain't doin too good. I'ma need you to help him out if he ask for it. Can you do that for me?"

"Yessir. What's wrong with him?"

"Nothin wrong with him. He ain't got no legs though. He in a wheelchair. And he ain't been in it that long. It got him down. So, can you do me that favor and help him out when he needs it?"

"Yeah, no problem."

"I knew I could count on you. You sho is a good boy. I wish mo people round here was like you. I'm tellin ya. If you can get this now, get this now and recover, the sky's the limit for you. The sky is the limit."

Part Three

I

Matthew sat pondering the unique tapestry that he had woven his life into. He had just finished *Of Human Bondage* and was currently thumbing through a stack of novels that Hugh had brought from his room for him to look at. He selected a James Michener. Setting it aside, he carried the stack of unchosen books through the door to the left of the bar and into the residential smoke-room. Soul music floated lightly through the room, radiating out from Hugh's door. Ty and David sat quietly smoking, absorbing melody, rhythm, and nicotine. Matthew knocked but no one came. Turning to the two he said, "Hey, if Hugh comes out, tell him his books are right there and that I got one."

"Alright," said Ty.

Going to return through the door which led back to the coffee-bar, David said, "Yo, pop a squat and kick it for a minute. Take a break."

The last meeting of the night was going on and it was unlikely that anyone would need anything, but Matthew propped the door open anyway so that he could watch the bar. He moved a chair so that he could sit and keep an eye on the till which was really just a kitchen drawer with a latch and padlock on it.

"Man, this job is just one long break. You do know that, right?"

"Really?" asked David, sounding jealous.

"Hell ya," said Ty, giving David a side-eye of skepticism for not having picked up on the laid back nature of the coffee-bar sooner. "I never see the people at the coffee-bar doin shit, no offense," he continued.

"No, you're right. Pretty much all I do is read and shoot the shit."

"Damn," uttered David. "I be slavin at my shit."

"Me too," said Ty. "Actually, I ain't gon lie. Drivin can be real chill. I just get me a big ol' thing of coffee and listen to the radio."

"Hey," Ty started up again after a moment's pause with the sound of having just had something pop into his head. "Did you know that John Cougar Mellencamp don't wanna be called John Cougar Mellencamp no more? He just wanna be John Mellencamp. Say he too old for the Cougar. Heard that on the radio yesterday. I don't think it's new news though. You know how everything get to us late."

The three sank into silence. They just listened calmly, smoking slowly, to the tune that poured from Hugh's room.

Ty and David were two of the people that Matthew spent a lot of time talking with since moving into the coffee-bar. The group that lived behind and above it was tighter-knit than many of the other houses, and had less turnover, especially than that of 1083. Downstairs were Hugh's single room and Matthew's shared room, and upstairs in the attic Ty and David lived with about ten other men in a poorly lit, low-ceilinged, slapdash bedroom. But complaints were rarely heard, most were just grateful to have a bed, given where many of them had come from, even if it was in a bug infested, raised dungeon.

Ty was a black man in his mid-forties, dark complected, with a neat mustache that clung closely to his upper lip. He was in great shape, due to his army days, and always wore tight fitting clothes that accentuated his physique. He was a truck driver by trade, and always wore a trucker hat over his completely shaved head. He was an outgoing country boy, and he and Matthew got along great.

David was a short Hispanic man with a goatee in his early thirties. He was somewhat standoffish by nature and even when he warmed up to you was still quite reserved. He worked as a sous-chef in a downtown restaurant. One reason Matthew gravitated to these two is because they both seemed to have their heads on straight, and that he always ran into them in the smoke-room.

Matthew heard the chanting of prayer coming from the meeting hall and put out his cigarette as it was 10 o'clock and therefore, time to close up for the night. Walking into the meeting hall as the last few people exited, Matthew saw the one person who was not allowed in there sitting in the corner, a caveman-like Asian man who had long, very matted hair, and was always wrapped in several layers of blankets no matter how sweltering it was outside. He looked like something out of the ice age. "Hey, you know you're not supposed to be in here. You gotta go. Get out." The man grumbled something incoherent and shuffled his way out the door.

Many homeless people came into the meeting hall and hung out either there or in the coffee-bar throughout the day, but Matthew didn't know why this man wasn't welcome. The coffee-bar was a place that sold stuff that the homeless could afford. The man never made any trouble, but Matthew assumed it was because he smelt absolutely rancid. 'If anyone needs help quitting, it's that guy.' Sometimes after kicking him out, Matthew brought him a small coffee out on the street just to show him that it was nothing personal. The man often took it as a token of peace and tried to reenter the meeting hall behind him. He felt like he had to treat the man like a dog since he knew no English and Matthew had to point with his finger out to the road and say "get." Though other times the man knew he wasn't allowed in and as soon as Matthew had turned his back, the man would attempt to stealthily infiltrate the hall like a child that's been told no but remains determined.

After clearing the meeting hall of its unwelcome presence, Matthew pushed all the chairs in, wiped the tables down, mopped the floor, cleaned the bathroom, changed the trash filled with Bob's lottery tickets, and locked the door. Returning to the bar, he counted the till. Even though he remembered counting out the coins on the floor of his mother's closet, something about them seemed to suggest an untapped memory, the rest of what happened that day. Every time he counted the change, his mind jumped with unconscious knowledge, but he always hit a brick wall in attempting to recollect exactly what it was. He shook his head with frustration and gave up.

'Eighty-four fifty, not bad. How many cups is that? If the small ones are a quarter and the big ones are fifty cents, and I sell about an even amount of them. But then I probably sold eight bags of chips and about the same in candy and those are a quarter a piece so then that's… easily over two hundred cups. How can we get away with selling the stuff the food-bank gives us? Maybe they don't care, it's nickels and dimes.'

Matthew put the money in an envelope and wrote *Matthew 5/10/13 p.m. shift $84.50* on it. He emptied his tip jar and counted out eleven dollars and thirty-six cents. Grabbing sleeves of small and slightly larger Styrofoam cups, Matthew replenished the supply next to the Bunn coffee maker. He then stocked the chip rack with the small bags of expired chips from the foodbank. He looked around one last time and concluded that he had done everything he had needed to. Sliding the tip money off the counter, he was thoroughly pleased. With the seven dollars and fifty cents on his dresser, he would have more than enough to smoke over the next two days he was off.

Matthew reached into the till drawer and pulled out Bob's envelope from the morning shift. It read *Bob 5/10/13 a.m. shift $46.* 'Why do I always sell more than him? I came through this morning for a cup, it wasn't that slow. How did he sell only forty-six dollars' worth of coffee? I mean, he's not very personable but still. I don't know, maybe that has something to do with it. Oh, well.' Matthew made his way next door to the office to deposit the day's envelopes.

Bob was a very tall and skinny white man, probably in his fifties. He had buzzed hair just around the sides of his head, and therefore was basically bald. He wore some of the longest jeans you ever saw, always with the shirt tucked in. He worked two jobs other than the coffee-bar, but his debilitating gambling addiction prevented him from ever being able to get on his feet. His job at the Home kept his rent paid and food in his stomach and so he could point to these things and say, "See I'm doing well. I'm taken care of.' But if he didn't scratch away everything he earned, he could have independence with his girlfriend instead of living years on end at an all-male transitional living facility or halfway house or three quarter or whatever you wanted to call it.

Matthew thought it sad how everyday he'd slink over to the corner store across the street, strutting almost, to lose anywhere from fifty to a hundred dollars. But that was okay because as he said he was just "one ticket away." Sometimes as he was scratching, he'd whisper to himself "this is the one, I can feel it." Matthew pitied the delusion that he had spun himself, and would ask, "how'd you fair today?" Not because he really cared but because he wanted to hear how this man could ratiocinate that winning twenty-five but losing sixty was coming out ahead.

Walking up the front steps, Matthew saw Duke sitting behind the desk reading. He didn't look up. He knew it was Matthew and so why interrupt his story. Matthew plopped the two envelopes down on the desk and hung around for a moment. Sighing, Duke set his book down and placed a pen at his spot. He spun the envelopes around and read the numbers silently. Grunting while he rose to deposit the money in the safe, Duke dully said, "You been makin a lot of money over there. Hugh's happy."

"Good, I'm glad."

"That makes one."

"What do you mean?"

"Wyatt and Bob, but especially Bob ain't thrilled."

"Why? Am I makin them look bad?" Matthew joked.

"Somethin like that," and Duke grunted again on his way to the office.

"Alright, well goodnight Duke."

"See you later."

Matthew made his way past the front desk and on his way to the gravel courtyard he heard the rusty noise of the safe's lever being spun around accompanied by the sound of the change within the envelopes clunking securely within.

Outside the wind blew and Matthew's head whirled. He had been roaming the streets at night in search of either the same woman from a few weeks earlier or one similar. His peripatetic routes were unplanned, other than the fact that he often went east into third ward, and he would slowly carve his way through the night streets hoping to find a woman, a beautiful woman, a beautiful woman that would exchange sexual favors for the measly pittance of small-faced bills and specie that jingled dejectedly in his pockets after a night at the coffee-bar. He had yet to find such a woman in his murky late-night movements but the thought, with no work the next day, called him like a siren. Regardless of whether or not his searches were fruitless, they did something for him. The idea alone would make him warm, producing a fleeting yet narcotic obsession that kept the notion of a worthwhile hunt alive. Occasionally, in the distance, a figure would move, and he would grow tepid conjuring images of seductively underclothed young women, but they never were. Almost invariably they were men, but the fatuous belief that a lovely and humane whore lie just around the next turn held him viciously. However, tonight his consciousness was somehow able to wriggle free.

Walking in through the alley backdoor, Matthew moved casually past the slow tunes to his own bedroom door which emitted a roar. Entering, it became deafening. Billy was the loudest snorer Matthew had ever heard. He slept with his bed against the back wall and two dressers blocking his view from the rest of the room though Matthew could sometimes hear him masturbate at night. Billy was a large, gruff man who generally kept to himself. He was neither tall nor particularly wide, but his paunch protruded enormously from the rest of his body.

Getting undressed and then in bed, Matthew looked first to his left to see *Of Human Bondage* and remembered it was due the next day, and then to his right to visually take in legless Willy. Willy was the sweetest old man, and he adored Matthew for always running to the store across the street to buy him Marlboro Reds, Duplex cookies, and two hotdogs with mustard and relish. Matthew knew that junk wasn't good for him; Willy was diabetic, but Matthew didn't think it his place to say anything. Willy knew it was bad; he had just had both his legs chopped off above the knee because of it. The thought of losing his limbs and going blind to future diabetes terrified Matthew. Willy had told him how only one of his legs had to go but after they cut it off, he became so depressed that he went back to the doctor and told him, "you might as well take the other," and so he did. That was eight or nine months ago. He could get in his chair decently though getting off the bed was a struggle. And he could roll around alright but none of the buildings at the Home were handicap accessible and so he often was forcibly confined to his bedroom. He could use his bedpan just fine but the task of dumping it in the attic toilet stood a staircase away. Matthew wasn't sure who dumped it but assumed it was Hugh.

Matthew stared at Willy. He had fallen asleep upright, pillows against the headboard behind him to prop him up so that he could watch the little portable black and white television on his dresser. He was milk chocolate complected, about seventy without any hair, and few teeth. His mouth hung open, and with his neck and head fallen uncomfortably forward, he drooled on his thin naked torso.

Next to Willy, on the sheets, lie a charred cigarette butt. He had done it again. Willy was allowed to smoke in bed since it'd be too difficult to lift himself in and out of bed all day to roll fifteen feet to the smoke-room but he sometimes fell asleep smoking. His medicine had that effect. The thought of the old wooden building going up in flames at night scared the hell out of Billy. He had discussed it with Matthew mentioning the dozen residents who lived upstairs. The thought of dying a fiery death frightened Matthew too but he used Willy's smoking to sometimes smoke in bed himself even though he was young, sprightful, and able-bodied.

Getting out of bed to cut off Willy's tv, Matthew momentarily gazed at him tenderly. He reminded Matthew of an angel, sitting there in his burn-hole covered bed sheets. Matthew threw the cigarette butt away, cut off both the tv and the lamp, and returned to bed. For a second, he curiously regarded Willy's painkillers. Sometimes, he left the bottle out which tempted Matthew. However, Matthew didn't see it tonight. For a minute, he playfully pondered as to where it might be. Shaking it off like he did the idea of loose women, he rolled over to face the wall and thought, "No, I couldn't do that. Not to Willy," and went to sleep.

II

It was the first day of June, Matthew didn't have work, and summer had begun to bloom. It was just after breakfast and Matthew sat out in the Serenity Garden drinking coffee and reading with George. He was just finishing Hugh's Michener while George ruminated on the day's devotional. Turning the last page, Matthew looked up through the Magnolia to a deep blue sky and then his vision faded to focus on the tree's smooth, silky, soft, white flowers blooming. George looked up to see Matthew was done.

"So, how was it, old boy?"

"It was good, real good. I never thought I'd know so much about Poland."

George chuckled. "That's why I love reading, you never know what exactly it's gon be about until you do it. Forces you to keep an open mind."

"Ya," responded Matthew contemplatively. "What was yours about?"

"Oh, this here. I read this every morning. Have for years. Nothin new except my perspective. Each year, I read these little daily scripts and no matter how many times I done read them, I see them in a new light. It's called *Jesus Calling*."

"But what's it about?"

"Well, I could tell you or I could just read it for you. This is actually yesterday's. Don't worry, it's short. It goes: 'The Peace that I give you transcends your intellect. When most of your mental energy goes into efforts to figure things out, you are unable to receive this glorious gift. I look into your mind and see thoughts spinning round and round: going nowhere, accomplishing nothing. All the while, My Peace hovers over you, searching for a place to land.

Be still in My Presence, inviting Me to control your thoughts. Let My Light soak into your mind and heart, until you are aglow with My very Being. This is the most effective way to receive My Peace.' There! Why don't you chew on that," and George rose to leave but before he did, he gently patted the book on Matthew's head.

'I guess I'll go to the library and maybe the park.' Matthew first went to his room to get his wallet, and on the way set Hugh's book down outside his door. Entering his room, he asked, "Willy, do you need anything?" Willy sat there eating a Nutter Butter. He reached for his pack of smokes, shook it, and determined it was relatively full.

"Oh, no no. I'm okay youngin. Thank you."

"Okay, I'ma head out. I'll be back in a few hours."

"Where you headed?"

"The library and maybe Hermann Park. It always looks nice, but I never been."

"Hermann Park," Willy reminisced. "Hermann Park lovely. Is it nice out?"

"It's beautiful. Want me to push you out?"

"Oh, no no. They got this special on. It's Clint Eastwood's birthday. He prolly at least ten years older than me. Anyway, they playin a lot of his old movies today."

"Cool."

"Speakin of birthdays, did I ever tell you about my last birthday?"

"No, you didn't. What happened?"

"Well, it was when my legs was startin to get real bad. And, over the course of about a week, my wife started to act funny. She'd say she was here or there but never had no receipts for nothin. And, it just started, and so I got to thinkin that she was two-timin my old ass. I just had this feelin. I didn't have no proof. But you don't need proof when you feel it in your gut. And oh, did that make me sick. And, I had had just about enough. I was sick, depressed, bed-ridden, waitin to have my legs chopped off, and now my wife got her something on the side and lyin about it. Uh-uh. Then it came one day where she was gone the whole day and I couldn't take it no mo. So, I grabbed my… I grabbed my… whatever it was, it was just like that Dirty Harry just had. You see that? So, I was in my chair at the time jus cuz it was easier than walkin and so I sat right there in the living room with the revolver in my lap waitin to blow her head off when she come through the door for foolin around on me. So, I sat, and I sat and about seven o'clock that night, I hear the key turn in the lock, and I don't just hear her, I hear a man with her. And I thought 'Oh you stupid bitch. I gon blow his head off too. Whatchu doin bringin him back here fo. To my house?' But then I hear other voices. Lots of em. I didn't know what was goin on. I wondered if the bitch was havin an orgy or something. And, I thought, 'you gonna do this under my roof?' But then she came round the corner and saw me sittin there with a bottle of whiskey and a handgun. This befo I knew what was goin on. And I don't know what it was that came over me but something on her face, when she came round that corner, just lit up. I had never seen nothin so beautiful. And, then she turned around and yelled, "come on in y'all he's up." And then all my friends and family come in. It was my birthday and I ain't even know it. I had been so consumed with drinkin and depression and pity. I had no idea. And I asked her why she been sneakin around the last week or so fo and she said it was cuz she been putting this whole thing together. Tryna keep it a secret. All for me. A surprise party. And to think, I was fixin to smoke her and whoever's ass came through that door with her until I saw that face," and he shook his head and his eyes watered. "Anyway, what you gon get to read at the library?"

"I don't know yet. Was just gonna look till I found something."

"I know what you should read. You should read this old book by this guy James… James something. Anyway, it's called picture or painting or portrait or postcard of a young man who's an artist."

"That's the name of it?"

"Yeah, somethin like that. It's real good though. I read it years ago. It's about a smart young man like you."

"Okay, if I can find it, I'll get it. Hopefully they have it."

"They'll have it."

"Okay, I'll check it out. I'll see you later Willy."

"Bye, Matthew."

Matthew walked to the train station, and after pretending to buy a ticket, got on the first northbound train. 'If I don't get my act together, I'm gonna end up like Willy. Old, legless, and drunk about to kill my wife. It really makes you that delusional. I was that delusional. Well, I can grow old sober. But what about my prediabetes? What does that even mean reversible? Isn't it that it either is or isn't? It was reversible a year ago, what about now? Is it too late? Oh, god. Am I gonna lose my legs and go blind eventually, one day…when I'm old? I won't be like Willy though because I won't have a wife. No one's going to want to marry me. Not when they find out that I'll be in a wheelchair and can't see one day. I want to find someone. But almost everyone drinks. Gotta find a sober girl. But how? Where? Meetings, I guess. Where else? And what does George's reading mean? Why did he tell me to chew on it? Is it personal, does it apply to everyone, or both? Transcend my intellect. My mental energy does just try to figure everything out, and God can see me spinning. And like it said it doesn't really do anything. I keep fighting life instead of just going with it. Don't struggle, trust. There was a lot of wisdom in that. I have to invite God in, if I want to receive peace. I want peace. I want to be content. I don't want to just be fighting everything all the time. I just want to be and be okay with just being. I just want to be in the now and be okay with being here in the now. I keep fighting and that's why I'm not in the now. I'm always somewhere else… wanting to be home. But if I just accept that I'll be here as long as I'm here, until God wants me somewhere else then it won't be a struggle because I'll have given in. Invite him. Invite him and know peace. Okay, here I go. God, I welcome you. Please take over what I think about. Please control what I do. I want the peace that I know only you can offer. There, that wasn't that hard.' The train came to a stop at Main Street Square.

Matthew headed west on McKinney. A peace had come over him. He chose not to focus on individual obscenities and instead looked at the value of the whole scene. 'It's life. It's ugly but there's beauty in it, beauty in that. The ugliness.' Walking up the library's walkway, Matthew saw the vagrants that hung outside not as homeless but as people.

Strolling inside, he asked a library assistant sitting behind a computer where he could find, "The Picture of the Young Man Artist."

"Uh, ah, *Portrait*, Joyce, yes. Hold on." She typed on the keyboard. Then she wrote 820.9 on the back of a used call slip and slid it to Matthew.

"Okay, thank you."

Circling through aisles, walking up and down stairs, Matthew eventually found the aisle. He found it odd that in this entire gigantic library, he should find it in the same aisle as *Catcher in the Rye* and *Of Human Bondage*. But he didn't give it too much thought. He returned downstairs to check it out.

"This is due back June 22nd."

"Okay, thank you."

Matthew walked back to Main Street Square on Lamar consumed with the idea of having God consume him. He ran the last block when he heard the approaching south bound train blow its horn. He got to the platform just in time, and he didn't bother pretending to buy a ticket. Luckily, no metro police were nearby.

On the train, Matthew decided to call his mother. She answered on the third ring.

"Hello," she said.

"Hi, mom. How are you?"

"I'm doing okay. What's going on honey?"

"Mom, I just wanted to say that I'm okay with however long I have to be here. I've been thinkin and I've realized that it's just going to take as long as it takes. I don't want to be any more unfair to you than I already have been or pressure you and try to convince you to let me come back when you're not ready. I'm okay with where I'm at. I have everything I need and I'm okay with how ever long it takes. I just wanted to tell you that."

"Well, I'm glad you said that. I'm relieved to hear you say that you understand that this is my decision and on my time. I've been worried that you'd never really realize that."

"Well, I do."

"So, how's the coffee-bar and front desk job?"

"It's good. I've been making more at the coffee-bar than anyone else. Hugh really likes me. I guess I already told you that when I got the job."

"How's your roommate? The older one."

"Willy, he's good. Me and him get along well. I feel bad for him though. He can't do much. He takes his medicine, but he just keeps doing what isn't good for him. You know, eating sweets and junk food. It's frustrating."

"Sounds similar to someone I know. It's frustrating to watch someone you care about destroy their life. It hurts, doesn't it?"

"Yes, mom," Matthew almost grumbled.

"I'm not trying to make you feel guilty. You're a caring and compassionate person and I know you already feel bad enough. I just wanted to point out the irony."

"I know and I do feel bad."

"I know. Hey, so I was thinking that since we both have weekends off that one of these weeks, I could come down there and visit you or you could maybe even, well we'll see how I feel about this later on but come stay one of those nights at the house. What do you think about that?"

"I would love to. If you picked me up on a Friday night when I got off at ten, I could spend all Saturday and Sunday with you. I would probably need to be back by Sunday night cuz I have work at six a.m. on Monday."

"Okay, like I said, we'll see. I still don't know when it'd be, but I think it'd be wise to ease you into coming home."

"Hermann Park, Rice U. Doors open left," said the automated voice through the train's speaker. Matthew stepped off the train.

"I think that's a good idea too. Hey mom, I love you, but I just got to the park. I'm gonna hang out here this afternoon. But I just wanted to call and tell you it's no rush. I'm content with where I'm at both physically and spiritually. I just want you to know that I'm okay with being here for as long as it takes."

"Thank you for saying that sweetheart. It tells me that you're starting to make some progress."

"Of course. Let's talk tomorrow and we can try to figure out when I can come visit."

"Well, like I said, we'll see when. But one of these weeks."

"Okay, I love you mom."

"I love you too honey, bye."

"Bye."

The park was packed. Everywhere people ran, jogged, walked, sat, lounged, hammocked, picnicked, hacky sacked, frisbeed, and played with dogs. Contented, Matthew walked alone on a pathway. He observed everyone, everyone around him, and most had other people with them. However, his solitude did not occur to him; he was happy seeing them, people he did not know, happy. For a while, he strolled leisurely while searching fruitlessly to find an unoccupied bench. He didn't have a goal and so winded an unplanned path that circled the park at a comfortable pace. After a full rotation of the trail, a couple on a bench not far ahead of him stood up and walked away. Unhurriedly, he claimed it as his own.

The bench sat facing a pond and Matthew watched the post-vernal sun glisten off the gentle motions of its ripples. Ducks in small groups glided softly across the water's inviting surface. Overhead, clouds delicately dotted the deep blue sky. Matthew sat lost in thought; he was at peace.

Throwing his arm over the bench and looking back, Matthew noticed many of the women moving about were relatively close in age. Many were very attractive, and he half seriously yet unabashedly looked upon their fit, firm, figures as they moved lightly about. It was a scene that in the past would have aroused a melancholy mindset but today his mood remained meditative. The contrast between the derelict figure on the bench and the charming women was striking. But while he did desire for someone to love him other than his mother, he sat assured. He remained not only seated on the bench smoking for random intervals but also confident in the notion that one day he would experience earnest romantic love to go along with the mended maternal. He sat for many hours, until dusk when the semi blind nutria stumbled clumsily out from the no longer sparkling pond, intimating his time of departure.

III

'The Home is to me as Clongowes was to Stephen. But I'm looking to return home, not leave. I don't know if that adds up,' Matthew thought as he sat behind the coffee-bar counter late one morning. He reflected on the Portrait book he had returned on its due date two days prior. The early morning had been busy as they always were, but it was unusually slow for almost lunch. Several people sat around at separate tables not talking but staring at their phones. A minute later, Matthew sat shocked when a familiar but nearly forgotten man strutted through the door. It was Alex.

"How ya doin bud?"

"I'm good. What are you doing here?"

"Came to see you. I had to drop some work stuff off downtown, and I thought I'd drop in and try to find you. Hugh over at the office said you'd be here. So, I see you got you a lil recovery job goin on here, right in the meeting hall. How ya likin it?"

"It's not too bad. Pays the rent."

"And I'm sure not much else."

"Nope."

"That's all you need right there. Three hots and a cot."

"Pretty much."

"So, I was hopin we could talk for a little bit. That fine?"

"Yeah, I'm just sittin here."

"Okay, well I gotta say, I've been worried about you. Last time we did work together was over three months ago and I ain't heard nothin since. So… here I am."

"Yeah, sorry about that. I've been busy."

"Too busy to do what you need to do to save your own life?"

"No, it's not like that. I've been doin good."

"Matthew," Alex began seriously. "You're a full-blown alcoholic living at a low bottom halfway house with three months sober. You can't possibly be doin that good. Perhaps starting to become institutionalized, like some of the guys that I'm sure have been crawlin around here for decades but certainly not good."

Matthew wondered how long he actually had been sober.

"You see me working. I've been talking with my mom about visiting and eventually coming home. I've been taking care of myself. Quite frankly Alex, you don't know what I've been up to," said Matthew defensively yet firmly.

"Well, tell me then. I'm sayin all this because I care about you, not because I'm tryin to hurt your feelings."

"I've been holding down a job here. They wouldn't have offered me the job outta everyone if I wasn't reliable and doing good. I've been talking to my mom and she agrees that I'm doing well. I help my roommate out who's wheelchair bound with just about whatever he needs. So, I'm helping others. I'm going to two to three meetings a week. Plus, I work here so I overhear a lot of meetings."

"Right, I don't believe they woulda given you a job here if you weren't noticeably improving but that's all short-term stuff. I'm talkin long-term growth, true recovery. The work."

"I work. I work every day. I do all sorts of work."

"But you know I'm not talkin bout that. I'm talkin about *the work*."

"If I do nine things right but fail to do one, does that mean

I'm doing bad?"

"All those things are great. They're essential to long-term recovery but you're failing to see that you're missing the foundational criterion of recovery. The work that is designed to bring about both a spiritual experience and transformation within you. Without that, everything else falls apart. Your assumption is that a job, meetings, staying sober, repairing relationships, etcetera are greater than or equal to the work that you know needs to be done. But those things can't replace the work with success. They're meant to be done in addition to, not instead of."

"Well, my mom thinks I'm doing alright."

"Matthew, your mother doesn't, I think, truly comprehend the nature of the beast that both she and you are dealin with. Do you remember about six months ago when I tried to talk to her about your alcoholism? She like you sees the severity of your illness, but she like you thinks that your ability to abstain from alcohol and drugs lies in your will power and how badly you want it. But you just can't wish alcoholism away by sayin 'you know what? I don't think I want to get drunk and high anymore' all willy-nilly and expect things to change. It doesn't work like that."

"Well, I've been praying. You're always talking about a relationship with God. What about that?"

"That's great. That's fantastic. But I got another one for you. 'Faith without works is dead.' You can't just petition God. He or she or it doesn't work like that. You can't just pay it lip service and expect things to change. You gotta do the footwork. Chop wood, carry water. Prayer is great but if it alone worked, how come God doesn't answer our 911 prayers? You know the type, 'Please God, if you get me outta this one I promise to' la-di-da. Tell me, if prayer in and of itself worked, how come all them people's prayers for world peace or to end hunger or poverty haven't paid off yet? I mean they're praying, right? They go to church and worship a god, right? How come it doesn't work then? I'll tell you why it doesn't work by itself cuz after you pray, you're supposed to take action. Every morning I pray to stay sober but then I get up off my ass and do what I know I need to do to fucking maintain it. Scratch that, grow in it which is helping others."

"But I told you, I help others."

"Yeah, but it's the last thing you do after you've done all the work. You're not there yet. I'm not sayin by any means don't help others. But I'm sayin that all the other pieces need to be done beforehand, in sequence, to produce the desired effect. You can't just choose elements at random that you like, discard the rest, and expect the magic to happen. You can't leave the eggs out when making a cake and wonder why it didn't come out right. You can't bake all the ingredients separate and say 'I don't know what happened. I had everything it specified.' There is a synergy that is made by doing the work in logical sequence. By following the directions."

"Okay, well what do you want me to do?"

"Did you reflect about everything we talked about last time I was here, like I asked, and then pray?"

"Yes," he paused hesitantly. "No, I didn't."

"Okay, well, start praying for God to take away your negative characteristics."

"Okay, I can do that," said Matthew begrudgingly.

"Good, and then we'll get started on rectifying your wrongs."

"What do I have to do there?"

"First, I want you to write down the names of everyone you've hurt or wronged. No matter how insignificant or trivial they may seem."

"Okay, but there's just some people that I'm not gonna say sorry to."

"Like who?"

"My father."

"Well, I anticipated that. I want you to pray for the willingness then."

"I'm not going to do that. I'm not willing."

"I know," Alex said calmly. "That's why you're going to pray to be."

"No, you don't get it. I'm not even willing to be willing. I don't want to be willing."

"Okay, we'll get to that in time. Meanwhile, we can get started on other people."

"Okay, how? I don't have a car. How am I supposed to meet and talk to these people?"

"You gotta phone, now don't you?"

"Yes."

"Well, give these people a call after you write up a written apology that I've looked over, and are then willing to own your actions."

"But isn't this supposed to be done in person? That's what I'm trying to say. How am I supposed to do that when I can't go meet these people in person?"

"Matthew, you would be amazed at what people are open to doing when they see us actively trying to better ourselves. And you don't know what God can make possible."

"I know the reality is most people aren't gonna wanna drive thirty or forty minutes to see me so that I can give them a bullshit apology. They're not going to believe me, that I'm sorry or even give me the time a day to begin with."

"You don't know that. And it doesn't sound like you're willing to set things right with anyone."

"No, what you're asking me to do isn't realistic. It can't feasibly be done at this point in time. So, why are you wanting me to stress over it? I can see all these people when I'm back home. I'll do it then."

"At the rate you're going and with an attitude like that, you won't be going home any time soon or ever. You know you could die, right?"

"I will be going home. I just don't know when. But it'll happen."

"Matthew, you're so young. You have so much potential. I

don't want to see you die from this illness."

"I'm not going to die. I'm fine."

"Why don't you just call me when you're ready?"

"I'm ready now. You're just not willing to work with me, with my extenuating circumstances."

"Yes, I am but you only want to do things your own way."

"Whatever."

"Call me when you're ready. I hope it comes soon."

"I'm doing just fine. I'm ready now."

But Alex didn't say anything. He just walked out worried.

IV

It was just before two o'clock and Matthew put his cigarette out in a cup that had just a little water in it on his nightstand. He sighed and sat up.

"Well, I'm about to go to work Willy. You want me to bring you a cup?"

"No, I might be in later though, just to get out."

Matthew put his shoes on and walked through the two doors, a distance of about twenty feet, and into the coffee-bar. The lounge area was busy. People sat around in groups talking, steaming little cups sat on the tables before them. Several people called out to Matthew, and he nodded and waved in return. Bob, who had his back turned to the bar because he was restocking the chip rack, looked over his shoulder.

"Hey Matthew, how's it going?"

"Good, what about you?"

"Oh, I'm alright, just tired. Would be better if you would learn to show up on time. On time is five before your shift, not right at two o'clock."

"My bad. Been busy?"

"Yeah, for a Thursday."

Matthew looked at the envelope on the back part of the bar with the morning shift's profit in it. It was full of cash but not sealed. There wasn't a dollar amount written on it either, just *Bob 7/18/13 a.m. shift*. 'That's odd. He's clearly counted it or else it wouldn't be in the envelope. Why would he go back later to write how much it was? And why does he sometimes take it over to deposit at the office himself and others he leaves it to me?' Bob finished stocking the chips, tucked the top flap into the envelope and said, "I'm off. Have a good day."

"Thanks, you too," said Matthew mistrustfully.

Bob took no notice of his suspicious tone and sauntered out the door to the meeting hall with his torso in front of his long legs and his head back. 'That's so weird. Why would he not total the envelope here? It's not like he's gonna go count it at the front desk again. I wonder if he's skimming some off the top. You know what, I bet he is. Oh my god, that must be how he has so much money to gamble. He must scratch several thousand a month, at least, between that and the Powerball. He's using the coffee-bar as his own personal piggy bank. He has to be. There's no other explanation. Between what I just saw and his gambling, definitely. And he didn't seal it. I would never. What a piece of shit. After all the Home has done for him. He's gonna repay it like that? I can't believe it. Here I am a thief and I never even thought about it. I didn't just steal from anyone like he apparently does. No integrity. Especially to a place that's done so much for him, for me. Right in plain sight. Under everyone's noses. The audacity. Wait. If he's gonna steal from the Home, he'd steal from me. Check the drawer. Cover my ass in case he shorted me.'

Matthew opened up the drawer. He counted a ten, a five, and ten ones. All of it was there. Knuckles knocked on the counter behind him. Spinning around, an old black man stood there. He grinned and said, "Can I get a big cup youngin?"

"Sure," said Matthew, mechanically grabbing and filling a cup and then setting it on the counter.

"Thank you very much," the man rattled off while slapping fifty cents down on the counter. The clang of the change struck him.

Matthew scooped the change up off the counter and looked at it in his palm. 'Did he touch my change?' As Matthew opened the drawer to both drop in his first sale of the day and inspect the number of coins, he dropped the quarters in their slot and swooshed the different denominations of change around with his hand. 'It all looks there.' The rustling of coins on the sides of the plastic till rang a bell. Not aloud in the coffee-bar but in Matthew's inner consciousness. He was swiftly transported.

Mark L sat across his kitchen table. A bag of quarters lay between them. Matthew swayed and had difficulty sitting up straight. The man looked at him wide-eyed, not sure of what to say. A minute or so of silence passed between the two.

"I thought you were sober," he finally said.

"I have been for the most part, lately, until today."

"What happened? I thought you were working with Alex."

"I am, I just, you know, got stressed out."

"Work?"

"No, I'm not currently employed."

"With what then?"

"You know, just life," Matthew said unconvincingly.

"I have to say," Mark L began uncomfortably. "I'm afflicted by the thought of giving you, an active drug addict, a large amount of money. It's conflicting. On the one hand what if you were to die. It doesn't matter to me that I don't know you all too well, I'd be devastated. It'd be hard for me to live with myself knowing that I supplied you with the financial means for that fatal dose of whatever. On the other, this is how I make my living. And it looks like it's going to be a hard year. The price of silver has dropped three and a half dollars per troy ounce in the last six weeks. I don't know if that means anything to you, at your current place in life, but that's ten percent in a little over a month and projections indicate that the market's going to tank this year. For me that means people are gonna be afraid to sell and the more people that hoard their coin and bullion waiting for the market to recover, the harder it is for me to provide for my family. So, the opportunity to acquire a sizable amount while the market is at a low spot is imperative but the fact that you're high just tears at me. I mean what if,"

"Oh," Matthew cut him off. "You think I'm gonna buy more dope, no. I already got it. I just need to pay the guy back. He fronted me."

"So, this is just to clean up a debt?"

"Exactly. I'm done doing dope. I just gotta get squared away with this guy."

"Oh, in that case, I'd love to do business with you." He picked up the plump plastic bag. "Now, how many did you say this was?"

"Eighty."

"Okay, I'll have to go through them and verify that they're all minted pre '65. And then I can pay you four dollars apiece."

"Four? You said five."

"I said I might be able to do five. But that was a week ago when you first reached out to me about these. The market's dropped since then. But I just can't with current market trends. Two months ago, I could have done six."

"Four and a half," Matthew countered.

"No," Mark L said firmly. "Since you're not going to get more drugs and you say that you're done with it all, I'll do four and a quarter. That's three hundred and forty and you're lucky to be getting that."

"Okay," Matthew grumbled.

Mark L poured the bag out on the glass table and started flipping the coins face up and after confirming the date slid them to a separate pile. While doing so he made small talk.

"So, where'd you get these?"

"My grandmother."

Mark L stopped and looked up in surprise.

"No, she left them to me. I didn't steal them," Matthew continued after he saw his reaction.

"Oh, okay, good. Well, these are all in good order," and he

pulled out a check book.

"What is that?" Matthew asked, irritated.

"You mean my check book?" Mark L asked, confused.

"No, I know what it is, but I thought I was getting cash."

"Oh, no, sorry. I didn't have time to stop at the bank. Matthew, what's your last name?"

"Wilkinson."

"Spell that."

"W-I-L-K-I-N-S-O-N, Wilkinson," he said slurring.

"Okay, here you go," he said, tearing it from his book. "It was a pleasure and I hope to both see you at some meetings sometime and do business again."

"Yep, I'll be there."

Matthew walked him to the door and shut it. He went to the fridge and grabbed two beers and sat with them on the living room couch, cracking one. He pulled his phone out of his pocket and saw that it was almost two-thirty. Leo was supposed to be there with the oxycontin by three. 'Perfect," he thought, having already forgotten about his sister and his mother. He took a long chug of his beer, belched, and then finished it. He threw the can to the side and cracked the other immediately while he slipped into profound relaxation just imagining how high he'd soon be.

Matthew was distant the rest of his shift. People would come to chat while they sipped their coffee, and he was largely capable of not much more than one-word responses. He thought of his mother, and how he had wronged her. More than anything, he wanted to make it right, to somehow get the coins back. He would do anything for her to forgive him.

'If I'm going to apologize to anyone, it's going to be her. When she finally comes to see me. It must be hard for her all alone. The one person she had betrayed her. She's done so much for me and I, I...' Tears started to well in his eyes. He held them back. He wanted to cry. He knew he could but thought 'can't be crying at the Men's Home.'

It wasn't busy that night, and when he closed up, he counted a profit of fifty-six dollars. Counting the change, he checked every quarter and thought perhaps he could overtime accrue eighty silver quarters and replace them with the regular ones from his tip jar. But there weren't any.

Closing up, he went to the office next door and was surprised to see Hugh sitting behind the front desk when he entered. Hugh sat reading but looked up when he heard footsteps approaching. Matthew instantly began to feel calm and serene in his presence.

"What are you doin working the front desk Hugh?"

"Oh, I do it occasionally if someone needs me to fill in. Dan couldn't make it tonight for some reason. How was today's haul?" he asked in his raspy voice.

"Not too bad, fifty-six."

"Boy I tell you, you made mo money for this place in jus a couple months than some of these no-good motherfuckers make in a year. How you do it?"

"I don't know. I guess I'm just friendly," he said as he thought about theft in its various forms.

"You smile, smilin go a long way," he rasped.

"Yeah, I guess."

"And you a salesman. You used to slang dope, right?"

"Yeah, just small time though."

"That don't matter. You got it in ya, entrepreneurship. You can apply that to anything. You entrepreneurs another breed. Jason sellin cars now. Who woulda thought? And now you sellin coffee ha ha. Would you have believed it a year ago if someone woulda told you you'd be sober and sellin cups of coffee now?"

"Probably not."

"But you is. Look at ya. I'm proud of you boy. You a hard worker. Not all, but a lot of these motherfuckers round here are lazy. But not you. You wanna know how much Bob made this mornin?"

"How much?"

"Thirty-eight dollars, thirty-eight," he said again, adding emphasis.

"Wow, not much."

"Damn right it ain't much. I walked through there this mornin too and it looked busy, but I guess people just don't like his attitude. He's not much of a people person like you. You know what I'm sayin?"

"Yeah, he can be alright sometimes though," Matthew defended.

"Alright sometimes ain't good enough if he drivin away customers with his shitty attitude. Anyway, I'm glad to have someone like you on my staff. Just need you to show these otha boys how it's done. Anyway, go turn in fo the night. I'm sho you tired. Just wanted to say how proud I am."

Matthew felt base thinking of his crime.

"Yeah, proud," he repeated halfheartedly almost to himself and then turned to leave.

V

It was a Friday night a few weeks later and Matthew sat behind the coffee-bar. It was quiet, and the few people that were in the bar were on their phones. Matthew had been talking with Jason for some time, but he had just left to go out with a woman. A few minutes later he returned.

"Man, you won't believe it. Someone stole my new ride."

"What?" Matthew asked.

"My new car, it's gone. I just went to get the keys off my dresser, and they're gone. I went out to the lot and it's not there either. Someone here stole it."

"I bet it was Tim," said Ty. "He been actin funny all day, like he smoked."

"Man, I swear to god. It better not be that motherfucker."

"Wait," said Matthew. "He stole your new car? Not his old one that you had?"

"No, I sold his old car back to him to get the down payment for this one. This is fuckin bullshit, I gotta call da police. Son of a bitch."

Jason stepped out on the phone.

"Ty, what makes you think it was Tim?"

"You shoulda seen that boy earlier, all geeked up."

"So, you think once he got his car back, he took Jason's new one to go sell?"

"Yeah, probably. The motherfucker's a crackhead."

"They said they got an officer on the way," said Jason reentering.

"What type of car was it?" Matthew asked.

"An '05 Impala."

Matthew felt funny.

"What color?"

"Silver."

'If it were gold, it would have been just like Leo's,' Matthew thought.

Abruptly his mind moved.

His phone buzzed. It was Leo. 'He's outside!' Matthew quickly downed the other beer. He approached the door and saw a car through the glass. He opened it and headed toward the gold Impala stumbling. He fumbled with the passenger side door handle for a second and then got in.

"You fucked up already?"

"I'm not fucked up. I'm just a little tipsy."

"You better not throw up in my car."

"I'm not."

"So, how many you want?"

"Can I get fourteen for three-forty?"

"No, that's less than twenty-five a piece."

"But you said you do deals for a lot of money."

"Yeah, I'll do em at twenty a piece if you got five hunid but you ain't got no five hunid so you gettin em at the full price."

"Thirty?"

"Mm-hmm."

"Come on man, I got almost three-fifty. Do em at twenty-five."

"I said no, motherfucker. You gettin eleven for three-thirty. I got ten change for you."

"Well, the problem is I got this."

"A check? You serious? You gettin ten for wasting my time."

"Whatever man, how do I do this?"

"Here," said Leo, tossing Matthew a pen. "Endorse the back of it where it says so and write 'pay to the order of Leo… You know what just sign it. I'll fill in the rest."

"Here," said Matthew, handing the check and pen over.

Leo pulled a pill bottle out from under his seat along with a revolver. He took a gram bag out of the center console and lightly tapped several blue oxy thirties into it, counted them, and added a few more. Matthew watched the pills fall lightly to be caught gently in the bag as if his life depended on it.

"There," he said.

Matthew counted with his fingers the pills in the bag, feeling each one through the plastic as he did so.

"Come on, throw in one more. There's forty extra bucks on that check."

"Here's a half. That's all you gettin you fuckin drunk junkie."

"What about the other twenty-five dollars on there?"

"Exchange rate. You makin me go to the bank. Now get the fuck out my car and hit me up when you want some hard."

Matthew got out and hurriedly walked up to his porch with a sudden swing in his step. He looked back for a second to see the gold shimmering car back out. Inside, he grabbed two more beers. Cracking one, he took three of the pills immediately. He staggered to his mother's closet, reached in the toybox, unscrewed the cap, and downed another alprazolam with his beer. 'I'll snort a couple of these and save the others.'

His mind then flashed back to Ty and Jason. He sat with them in silence. About twenty minutes later, someone up front in the meeting hall called out, "Somebody call the cops?"

"Yeah, tell em to come back here," yelled Jason.

A minute later an HPD officer entered. He was white, young, tall, and had his black hair neatly parted down the side.

"Who called?" he asked authoritatively.

"I did," said Jason, stepping up.

The officer's right hand instinctively moved towards his holster as Jason approached.

"You need to keep your distance, alright? Alright?"

"Alright," muttered Jason.

"Now, what's the problem?" he asked.

"My car was stolen."

"What's your name?"

"Jason Lenoir."

"I'm gonna need you to run a check on a Lenoir, Jason," he radioed.

"Whatchu runnin my name fo? I didn't do nothin. You ain't even get the info on my car yet and you talkin bout runnin a check on my name n shit."

"That's for my safety. You don't need to worry about what I do for my safety. All you need to do is to do what I say."

"Okay," Jason conceded.

"Have anything on your person I need to know about? Any drugs, guns, or illegal substances?"

"What? No."

"Put your hands on your head and spread your legs."

"What? Why? I didn't do anything."

"Just do what he say," said Ty.

"Why you bothering him?" said Matthew. "He called y'all."

"Mind your business," the officer said, turning to Matthew. "Now you got anything sharp that's gonna stick or poke me?"

"No, I said no."

Feeling up and down his pant legs the officer said, "What's this?" and pulled out a condom. "I didn't think you was like that," he said.

"Like what?"

"Homosexual. But you see something new every day on the force."

"What the fuck are you talking about?"

"You, I'm talking about you. A gay gangster. It's unusual."

"What are you even talking about?"

"You, walking around the Men's Home with a condom. This where you get your action?"

"That's fo a female n you know that. Why y'all always tryna falsify the black man's public image? You wrong fo that one."

"Cuz they scared of what we could be if they let us get up on they level," said Ty.

"Shut the fuck up. I ain't scared of nothin," said the officer to Ty.

"Caulder, we got nothin on a Lenoir, Jason," came the radio.

"Copy," he responded. "Alright, you're good. Now what happened?"

"Now, what I was sayin was, befo all that jus happened was that my car was stolen."

"Make and model?"

"Chevy Impala."

"Color?"

"Silver."

"Year?"

"'05"

"Plates?"

"I don't know. I just got it. They was temporary ones."

"Do you have the title?"

"In the car."

"Was it in your name?"

"Not yet. I was about to get it switched over."

"If we find the vehicle, is there any way you can prove that it is in fact your vehicle?"

"If you call the man's name that's on the title, he'll tell you he sold it to me."

"Okay, good enough."

"Do you think y'all'll find it?" asked Jason.

"Probably not."

"Damn."

"Anything else for me?"

"Well, the keys were taken. It wasn't hotwired. So, we know it was someone here."

"Oh, so, you think you're a fucking detective now?"

"I didn't say that. You asked me if I knew anything else."

"So, who here do you think took it then?"

"I don't know."

"Maybe this guy Tim," Ty said. "He was being real sketchy earlier."

"Know his last name?"

"Rodero," said Matthew.

"Is that it? That all y'all got?"

"Yeah," said the three.

"Okay, we'll be in contact, if we find anything out."

"Alright," said Jason.

"Say, give me a cup of coffee," said the officer addressing Matthew.

"Sure, that'll be fifty cents."

"You're kidding me."

"Nope, if the homeless can afford it, so can you."

"You getting smart with me? What's your name?"

"Matthew Wilkinson."

"I also need you to run a Wilkinson, Matthew," he radioed again.

"What makes you think I did anything wrong?"

"You're just the type, defiant. Not to mention you're clearly a drug addict living here. And losers usually have records."

"Defiant? Cuz I didn't give you a free coffee? You didn't exactly come in here peacefully," retorted Matthew.

"You want to talk about peace? I keep the peace against thugs like y'all. I serve and protect. I put my life on the line every day."

"Nothing on a Wilkinson, Matthew," rang statically through the bar.

"No, you do the opposite of keep the peace," began Matthew. "Y'all are society's most disgusting, disruptive, and arbitrary force ever. I'm tired of the phony image that y'all put forth and that white America just eats up, that y'all are heroes. You're not. It makes me sick. Y'all are the thugs. Y'all're bullies with inferiority complexes, treatin Jason and me like this. You should be ashamed. Protect and serve? That's the biggest joke I ever heard. You want a free cup of coffee? You want to be treated like a hero? Go do something heroic. Go find Jason's car. If not quit harassing us."

The officer stood akimbo and hocked a loogie on the floor and left. Ty, Jason, and Matthew were the only three left in the room now. They looked at each other for a minute in relief.

"Man, fuck that guy," said Ty.

"For real," said Matthew.

"Dawg, I appreciate you sayin that. I wanted to say something but he woulda had my ass on the way to County on some bullshit if I did," said Jason.

"No problem, anytime," responded Matthew.

"I mean it's a privilege. Don't get it twisted," started Jason. "Bein able to talk to the law like that. But you did the right thing. Used it the right way. You didn't cuss at him. You didn't raise yo voice at him or nothin like that. He woulda had yo ass on the flo if you did. You jus spit straight facts. He couldn't even argue either ha. He jus left. That motherfucka prolly mad as hell right now in his car drivin all fast n shit lookin fo somebody else to fuck with."

"Probably," agreed Matthew.

"Nah but on some real shit. On a serious note, I wish mo white people yo age was like you. Forget the old folks or even yo parents, they ain't changin. But I wish mo was like you cuz the level of racism that yo kids n my kids gon have to deal with isn't really gon be determined so much by how the black community fights racism but how white folk yo age stand against it. They listen to y'all, not us. They always tryna control how people see us. Like I told him. Push us to the edge n shit and then say, 'see, look how they act.' They try to make us out to be thugs and what not. He tried to say I was gay. Not cuz he believed it but cuz he would then control my image or even worse how I see myself. They kill us not fo what we really are but fo what they say we is. Ain't that a bitch? America racist as hell but I'm glad to know we got some white folk, like you, that see it fo what it is."

"Of course, man," replied Matthew knowing nothing further needed to be said.

"What time is it?" asked Jason.

"About nine-thirty," said Ty.

"Well, I'ma go call that woman and hit the hay. She prolly mad as hell. Prolly think I stood her up on purpose. But I'll jus tell her what happened."

"You gon need a ride to work in the mornin?" asked Ty.

"Either that or catch the bus," said Jason.

"I gotchu after breakfast," said Ty.

"Bet."

That night Matthew roamed the streets. He had told himself that he only wanted to clear his head after the memory of buying from Leo, and the argument with the officer took place but he quickly found himself looking for feminine figures in the night. His mind played tricks on him. Every time he first glimpsed a shadow walking, for just that first brief instant, his subconscious projected an idealized feminine profile that quickly evaporated into whoever it really was. He wanted to feel in control the way he had in addiction, like the way he had when he told that officer off and the way he had for just those few seconds. 'In eleven days, that will have been four months ago. My birthday.' Even though he knew all that control was an illusion, he still chased it. It still felt very real in the moment. He wanted to both forget and relive the experience. 'How does one think no more of and feel something at the same time?' He did not know. And so, he solemnly walked in the half glow of the streetlights, troubled with thoughts of his life that all circled back to his mother, while imagined shadows of real people danced hauntingly around him in the eternal light of that warm August night.

VI

The days came and went but no longer blurred together like they had the first several months Matthew was at the Home. It was the weeks that Matthew now had difficulty differentiating. There was something deep about the Home that seemed to escape time. Matthew was well aware of this, and he stood still with time as the world outside evolved and transitioned.

However, as his unpleasant dreams faded away, it seemed so too did a handful of the neighborhood's fixtures.

The surrounding Midtown area was undergoing a transformative process aimed at beautifying the area, raising property values, and attracting higher paying tenants with the installation of chic clothing stores, upscale restaurants, and trendy bars and nightclubs. But the Home stood unchanged. It had survived multiple phases of gentrification. What was one more? At least that's what the residents thought until one day when Hugh announced that the Home was to be purchased by the city. It was to be transitioned into a co-ed drug and alcohol rehabilitation facility that they proudly announced would be need-based as if the current residents were presently living beyond their means.

To the west of the office building across the light-rail tracks a new luxury apartment building, that was just a construction lot when Matthew first arrived appeared as though it was starting to near completion, and the city was to build a new modern Men's Home just across Fannin from 1083 to the east. There was to be a ceremonial ribbon cutting done at the lot where the new Home was to be erected on Saturday August thirty-first and Hugh asked Matthew if he'd like to make a few extra bucks parking cars for city council members, planners, and donors who would be in attendance, but Matthew declined. He'd be going home, for the first time, to visit for the weekend.

The Friday night before the big event, Matthew turned in the coffee-bar envelope and sat nervously on the front steps of the meeting hall waiting for his mother's car to arrive. He was both excited and anxious. Excited because he'd be spending time with his mother. Anxious because this whole visit was a test and would decide when he could leave the Home, and go back to his own, for good. He anticipated that part of the test would be to have a long, serious talk about his behavior and his mother would gauge his preparedness by how well he handled owning his actions. And so, he sat with mixed emotions for her to arrive, but his contentment certainly far outweighed his fear.

A few minutes later, his mother's car pulled slowly up to where he sat. He took a deep breath, grabbed his backpack, and got into the car. She greeted him warmly, and they embraced momentarily. The car began to move and, on the way home they talked casually. Matthew was elated and he tried with effort to manage his emotions and control the words that wanted to gush forth from his mouth in a torrent. His mother clearly missed him too and sat driving with a calm smile that betrayed utter fulfillment.

They reached their home, and inside their chihuahua jumped at his sides to affectionately greet him. It was almost eleven and his mother was worn out from getting up at five-thirty that morning for work. But she stayed up another hour or so watching tv with Matthew. They used to watch tv all the time together, and it was like he had never even left but at the same time it was all so different. Good but different. He wasn't insanely drunk while he sat with her now and he was so unaccustomed to it that it almost made him feel uncomfortable. Sobriety at the Home was one thing but returning to his old stomping grounds in a sober frame of mind struck him as incredibly surreal. After his mother went to sleep, Matthew lay awake for another few hours with one of their two cats at his feet and their dog nestled cozily at his side.

In the morning, Matthew rose from the couch when his mother came out of her room. For breakfast she made them cheesy eggs, sausage, and toast. They ate it together quietly reading, and overcome with happiness, nothing needed to be said. Matthew read *Sons and Lovers*, something he had found on the same shelf as his previous three library selections. He found it to be startlingly relatable while his mother read something she had seen on Oprah's Book Club years ago that she thought was incomprehensibly relatable to her son's rehab experience though it had later come out as fabricated.

They spent the whole day together reading, playing with the pets, sitting in the yard, and watching funny television shows. It was fantastic, and so it was with genuine surprise that Matthew looked on as his mother that night nonchalantly popped open a bottle of beer. Noticing his startlement, she simply said that she would like to be able to enjoy a few beers. It didn't immediately distress Matthew as he knew he couldn't expect everyone to change because of him. A little later she said, "you know I wish being able to have and enjoy a beer was something you were able to handle."

"I can handle a beer."

"You really think you can?"

"Yeah, I haven't had one in five and a half months. Wow, I can't believe that I've been gone almost six months."

"Okay, but you are not drinking all my beer. You can have a few, relax, we can order some Chinese food and have a nice night. I've missed you; it feels so nice yet almost strange to have you back. Even if it is just for the weekend."

"I've missed you too mom, so much. More than I can put

into words. More than you can imagine. It just feels so good to be back with you and the pets."

"Believe me, I want to have you here. I don't like to think of you being down there alone. I miss having you with me. That's why you need to learn to take it easy on those things. When you get a nice buzz going that's when you need to be able to just say no and chill and enjoy it."

As it hit his lips, he loved it. He felt as if he had been reunited with an old friend much like he had when his mother first picked him up the night before. He instantly grew warm and found it cumbersome to take small sips but he forcefully managed. It took every ounce of self-control within him to not toss the entire bottle back right then and there. Though he had everything he could ever want or need right in front of him, mainly his mother, he pined to intensify this fuzzy feeling.

That night Matthew painfully limited himself to just three beers. When she went to bed, he laid awake wishfully thinking of the few bottles left in the fridge but abstained. The next day they relaxed just as they had the day before. And it was with bitter feelings that Sunday night that he rode back down to the Home with his mother.

They made this their weekly routine. Every Friday evening at ten, after closing up the coffee-bar, his mother would pick him up. They would relax and watch tv that night, order food and have a few beers the next, and she would return him to the Home on Sunday. Matthew loved it, and it was by far the part of his week that he most lived for. Though every week it got harder and harder to moderate. Somehow, he managed to, except for one night when after his mother went to bed, he polished off the four bottles left in the fridge. After doing so, he thought about taking her car quickly up the road to the store to buy some more, not much, but more. However, he realized that she had taken her purse to bed with her, a hitherto unseen move. Matthew even thought about slyly creeping into her bedroom to retrieve her keys and then returning them later. But he decided against it. Besides, it was probably for the best.

VII

On Saturday, three weeks after the ribbon cutting ceremony, Matthew's mother came down to see him, not to pick him up for the weekend but rather to spend the day with him. She had been invited to a friend's house the night before and told Matthew that she couldn't pick him up that night but that they could spend that Saturday together instead. In the past this would have greatly saddened Matthew, the idea that his mother would prefer to spend time with someone else rather than himself. And now, while it didn't unbelievably bereave him of joy, he was somewhat disappointed at missing out. However, he wanted his mother to be happy and have friends.

They were going to go to Hermann Park for the afternoon. It was just after lunch, and Matthew's mother called to say that she was parked outside in the gravel lot. Matthew went out to the car and for the short ride to the park they talked casually. He was nervous because today he was going to make a formal apology to her not only about stealing her coins but also for his general poor behavior over the last five or so years. He hadn't talked to Alex about it but had mentioned it to Ty and David and they suggested writing it down in case he started to stumble over his words or totally forgot what to say. As they pulled into a parking spot, Matthew felt the firmness of the tightly folded sheet of paper in his pocket. He was growing more anxious by the second.

For a while, they strolled leisurely through the park. It had rained heavily early that morning and this had almost caused them to cancel the day's plans but after a few hours of only cloudy weather they decided to go through with it. However, during their shaded walk, it remained excessively humid and warm with the possibility of a downpour looming over their intimate outing.

Matthew's mother sensed something heavy on her son's mind, and when they took a seat at a bench, she asked what was going through his head.

"Mom, there's something that I want to talk to you about."

"What is it honey?"

He took out the sheet of paper but didn't unfold it.

"Mom I feel horrible about what I did, stealing your coins, grandma's coins. When I did it, I wasn't in the right frame of mind. I was sick. But that's no excuse. I want you to know that I deeply regret what I did. And I hope you know that I would never do that the way I am now, in this condition, sober. When I did it, I was only thinking of myself, of what I could get, of what I wanted. I was being selfish. At the time, I didn't care where I got the money to get high. I didn't care who I stole from or hurt whether it was something from grandma or you or anybody for that matter. It was all about me. And that's how it's been for a long time. Over the years, I've been dishonest and manipulative in order to feed my addiction. I don't want to make excuses but what dad did to us, to you, really fucked me up. Anyway, you're the last person in the world that deserved that, especially coming from me. Ninety percent of the time everything is fine between us. I'm talking strictly about our relationship, not anything that goes on in our lives or happens to us, but ninety, ninety-nine percent of the time we're fine. I just mess up every now and then and this time I messed up big.

But I want you to know that I've been saving up, and I'm going to get the coins back. I have almost half the money. Anyway, I love you so so much. And it hurts me to know that I've hurt you. That I've lost your trust. I never want that to happen again. I never want that or anything like it to happen again. And so, that's why I've been working on myself. I want to do whatever it takes to make it up to you. What do I have to do to repair our relationship? And did I forget anything?"

"Matthew, I don't know where to begin. The thought that you think that sort of apology will cut it just baffles me. I mean, how delusional are you? To begin with, I already got the coins back a few weeks ago. I went through your phone. Do you know how much it cost me to get my own stuff back? Four hundred and forty dollars. I don't know how much that Mark gave you for them but that's what he charged me. And then, before that, when I thought it was that Leo guy that I saw in your phone who sold you all of whatever, I called him, and do you know what he said he was going to do to me? He said he was going to rape me. Rape me! I don't know who this motherfucker is, but I told him that if he came over that I was going to blow his fucking head off. So, now I have to deal with that. The fear that somebody is going to come over to my own home and try to rape me. And that's all because of you and your addiction. You've got some nerve going through my closet to get those. Those were my mother's! You're always going through my stuff, looking for those pills. I swear those are all you care about. Do you know how much of one of those I take at a time? A quarter, a quarter! Sometimes a half. But you. You gobble up handfuls. I honestly don't know how you're alive. You should be dead. Do you know what it's like to constantly worry that your child is going to die? Of course, you don't. You have no idea the hell I've put up with so that you can be fucked up all the time. It's all at my expense. Everything. Every time. How can you sit there and say that we're fine ninety, ninety-nine percent of the time? Yes, most of the time we get along but that's because you're always out of your fucking mind and I put up with it. I just put up with it. On the off chance that maybe you'll realize that that's no way to live. But I'm obviously the fool. Because I just keep letting it happen. And there, I blame myself. I just let it happen. You have no idea what it's like to constantly blame yourself for your child's behavior, for their horrific drug addiction. It must be my fault. I see your old childhood friends doing well, and I see their mothers and think 'what did they do that I didn't. Where did I go wrong?' Those are the things I ask myself. And you should just see yourself. I can't understand what you're saying half the time. Mumbles. You just mumble. Just mumbling like 'mwa mwu mwa mwa mwu mwa want me to make some pancakes?' You have no idea what it's like to put up with that. To put up with the fear that if you leave the house, you're going to die or end up in prison. So, I let you drink and do whatever the hell it is that you do that gets you like that. I let you do that at the house not because I'm a cool mom but because I'm scared shitless of what's going to happen to you. At least under my roof, I can keep an eye on you, but this is the price I pay for it. This is the price. And you ask, 'is there anything else?' Like you've even begun to scratch the surface. My car, your car, totaled. All the times I had to bail you out of jail. Running around with guns. The shit you break on a daily basis when you fall or drop or bump or knock over my things. My nice things. You've really done a number on me. I can't afford to have you go on like this, emotionally, financially, mentally. I can only take so much. And you want to make things right. It's going to take a longtime, a lifetime. You want to make things right? I want to see you succeed. I want you to do well and be happy. And I know you want to be happy. I know that. I know that part of the reason you get so trashed is because you're unhappy. You're doing good now though. I want to see you grow and flourish into the man that I know you can be. That I know you are, deep down inside. I wasn't planning on going off on you like this, but I needed to say it, you needed to hear it, it's been a long time coming. I do love you. You mean the world to me. And I know you meant well with your apology, but I just couldn't sit by and shake my head and say 'it's okay sweetie. Everything's fine.'

Matthew sat stunned. He didn't know what to say. There was so much for him to process. The only identifiable action that came to his head was to start crying. He wailed on that park bench with his face in his hands, unable to look his mother in the face for the shame he felt, as the storm clouds overhead grew darker. The park had started to clear out at the sound of thunder, and Matthew's mom suggested they do the same.

On the way to the Home, out of nowhere she said, "You know, I was thinking that maybe you could come home right before Christmas."

"Really, for good?" asked Matthew teary eyed.

"Yeah, really. That's only three more months. You'll have been there nine by then, and I was thinking that that's probably long enough."

"Thank you, mom. Thank you, so much. I love you. I really am really sorry for everything."

"I know you are sweetie. I know you are."

VIII

It was dinner time and Matthew sat behind the front desk. For the last hour, a long line of homeless men and women gathered outside to get a hot meal. The line now went down the block and wrapped around the corner. Matthew prepared for the short speech that he gave to the homeless every Wednesday prior to letting them in. He took a deep breath and headed down the half flight of stairs to outside.

"Alright y'all listen up," he commanded. "I know all y'all are hungry. I know y'all been waitin in line for an hour or so. But before I can let y'all in to eat, I gotta go over some ground rules. They ain't new to y'all, I know y'all hear them from Duke or Dan or me or Hugh everyday but still, this is important so pay attention. Absolutely no drugs or alcohol are allowed on the premises. This is a zero-tolerance policy. If we catch any of y'all with drugs or alcohol, you're out, gone. Not just tonight but for good. I'll point you out to Chef Davy and he'll make sure you never eat another meal here again. That being said, no yelling, fightin, funny business or anything like that. Y'all know how to act so just behave. As y'all know, I can only let five of y'all in at a time. So, eat quick cuz there's a whole lotta other people waitin patiently outside for their turn. Those are the rules. I expect y'all to follow them."

Having finished his regular Wednesday night speech, Matthew wasn't surprised to look around and see very few people actually looking at him and even they stood unlistening. However, he was surprised to see about twenty people back a man take a sip from a forty ounce malt liquor bottle, screw the cap on, and stick it back in his backpack. Since getting relatively sober, Matthew learned that he did not enjoy confrontation, and that the old aggressive attitude of his was really just the manifestation of chronic alcoholism. He momentarily shuddered but went to approach the man.

"Hey man, that bottle in your bag, you can't bring that in. I just gave a speech about it. It was the first rule."

"Oh, yeah, what are you gonna do about it?"

"Look man, don't make me be the reason you don't eat tonight. Just get rid of it, okay?"

"Well can I at least finish it? I bought it," said the man drunkenly.

"I'm really not supposed to but go ahead and finish it if you must. When I come back out, I better not see it again."

"Will do, boss," the man chuckled.

Walking back to the front door, Matthew motioned for the first five in line to come in. They did so, marching quietly to the dining hall. Matthew resumed his seat behind the desk and leaned back, the chair rolled unevenly. He was told that roughly thirty years ago, a man who worked the front desk scratched lottery tickets there until his death. It was his lottery shavings, rolled over an innumerable number of times through the years, that were matted into the almost inch thick black mat at the foot of the front desk that now caused Matthew's seat to be wonky.

"Five more," yelled Chef Davy from the kitchen.

Matthew went to let five more people in. On his way back up the stairs, the phone rang.

"Men's Home," said Matthew, answering.

"Ty?"

"Yeah, I'm here. But if you want to talk in privacy, I'd wait until after dinner."

"Till ten."

"Okay, see you later."

Matthew went out to get another round of hungry people. He watched as they entered to make sure that none of them went into the restroom and stole all the toilet paper or soap or anything like that. 'I wonder what's up with Ty. He sounded nervous. I hope he's okay. What could he have wanted to talk about?' Just then the phone rang again.

"Men's Home."

"Jerry?"

"What do you mean you're in jail? Which jail?"

"No, I can't. The Home can't bail you out. Especially if you can't even tell me what for. I don't think the Home will do that."

"What'd you do?"

"If you want me to help, you gotta tell me."

"A woman. What kind of woman? Oh."

"Yeah, I see. Right, a mix up."

"Well, even if it was a case of mistaken identity, I don't think the Home can put up bail for you."

"Uh huh."

"Hugh? No, he's not here."

"I mean, I guess I can get him. I'll have to put you on hold."

"Okay, I'm gonna call him. Hold on."

Matthew placed the phone on hold. He went out front to let five more people in. The man that had had the malt liquor bottle came in in this group. Matthew returned to the desk, put the phone up to his ear, and took it off hold.

"Jerry, you there?"

"Yeah, no. I tried twice but he didn't pick up."

"What? No, I'm at the front desk right now. It's dinner. You know I can't just leave while we're feeding the homeless and go knock on Hugh's door."

"Yeah, I guess."

"When it dies down, I'll go."
"Yeah, of course. In the meantime, I'll keep calling him."
"Okay."
"Okay."
"Hang in there."
"Yes, I'll get him."
"Okay, bye."

Matthew put the phone down confused as to why Jerry would think that the Home would bond him out with such a ridiculous story. He got up and took a few steps over to peer in the dining hall door to make sure everything was orderly. Surveying the room, he first saw a malt liquor bottle hidden covertly under a table by someone's feet. His eyes followed the feet up the body to see the man whom he had given a warning to outside. Enraged at the thought of this man flouting not only the rules but also his friendly warning, Matthew approached the man from behind. He had only taken a few bites of his meal when Matthew, without saying anything, reached from behind him, grabbed his tray, and dumped it in the trash.

"What the hell, man?"

"Get out," said Matthew.

"What the fuck's your problem?"

"I told you not to bring any liquor in here. I tried to be friendly but instead you just disregard the rules and endanger everyone here trying to stay sober. Get out."

The room was quiet. Everyone looked on. Chef Davy stopped serving, and walking out of the kitchen said, "He's right. It's time fo you to leave."

The man picked up the glass bottle and squared his shoulders with Matthew. He thought the man was going to swing the bottle at his head and so he slowly backed out to the lobby, never taking his eyes off the man or the bottle. When he had backed up to the entry staircase and pointed his hand out over it signaling one last time for the man to go, the man lowered his head and charged. The top of his head hit Matthew square in the chest which sent him falling powerfully back over the six steps. The force from the blow caused him to clear the steps and he landed painfully on his back. The man walked drunkenly down the half flight, passed Matthew, and out the door. Matthew lay aching on his back, his body reeling from both the hit and the impact of the fall. He heard Chef Davy on the phone with the police. David, who he had seen eating quietly in the corner, helped him to get up. Matthew staggered up the steps and plopped down into the old office chair. Chef Davy went down the steps and out the front door to address the hungry crowd waiting.

"Ain't nobody else eatin in my kitchen tonight," he said toothlessly. Yells in protest were heard. "Oh, you don't like that, make it a week." More yells were heard but this time with insults. "That's fine, that's fine. I really don't care how you feel about me. The police is on they way. But while y'all're hungry every night this week, I want y'all to know it's all cuz of that man right there," and he pointed before coming back inside.

Chef Davy brought Matthew a cup of water and a few minutes later two white HPD officers arrived. They rushed in with their guns drawn. "Get on the ground. Get on the ground! Hands behind your head." One officer pointed a gun a Matthew's face while the other went into the kitchen and ordered everyone eating to get on the floor. The officer by Matthew and Chef Davy asked, "Where is he?"

"He went out the door. I told y'all that when I called."

"I'm gonna light his ass up," said the officer by Matthew running out into the evening sun.

The second officer walked into the lobby and asked what happened. Chef Davy explained as Matthew was still shaken up.

"Is this true," he asked Matthew.

"Yes."

"What'd he look like?"

"I don't know," began Matthew. "He was black, maybe thirty-five, wearing a black jacket and grey sweatpants."

"How tall?"

"Maybe five-ten."

"Keep your eyes out for a black man wearing a black jacket," he radioed in.

"So, tell me again what happened."

Matthew repeated the incident as Chef Davy had already explained.

"Would you like to press charges if we find him?"

"No, it's not a big deal," said Matthew wearily.

"That's okay, the state will probably pick up charges."

"Myers, I need back up. I have the suspect at gunpoint. Main and Cleburne. Black male, black jacket, red basketball shorts," came through fuzzily.

"That's not him," he radioed back and ran out the door.

Matthew was shaky that entire night. More so from having a gun pointed at his head than from being headbutted down half a staircase. He sat turning both incidents over in his head, thinking of what he could have done differently with each scenario to have prevented their outcome. With the homeless man, he concluded that he shouldn't have backed up to the staircase, but he would have probably been struck in some way regardless. 'But with the police there wasn't anything different I could have done. That's just what they do. Make a subset of the population fear for their lives and then convince everyone that they save lives. They're the real threat. Fucking gaslighters. I wonder if that poor guy who they thought it was is alright. Terrorize him and probably high-five each other, go home and beat their wives.'

About nine-thirty that night, the door opened, and Ty came in. He looked terrible. His eyes were sunken in, there was something unusual with his healthy dark color, and he wore an expression of defeat. He took the seat across from Matthew, rubbed his forehead, took off his hat and when he did the dull light reflected off his bald head. Ty looked around to make sure no one was close by.

"I fucked up, man," he started.

"What happened? Did you use?"

"Yes, man. And I'm scared."

Seeing this usually outgoing and happy, buff man reduced to utter fear scared Matthew.

"Okay, tell me what happened."

"Last week, I was drivin this covered wagon up to Fort Worth, right. I'm gonna be honest, I stopped at a bar."

"Okay, so you drank?"

"No, well yes but I wasn't done yet. At the bar, I start talkin to this lady, right. And she got some coke. So, we go out to the parkin lot to do it. But when I do it, it just piss me off. Cuz it wasn't enough to make me feel how I wanna feel, right. So, I ask her if she know anywhere I can get some rock, right. So, she takes me to this dude, and I get a hundred sack off him. And so, I laid up in the motel smokin that with her all night. We finish it and I say I'm done, right. That's it. No one will know."

"So, it's been about a week since you smoked?"

"No, you didn't let me finish. So, I been fightin the urge. Fightin the urge all week prayin, right. But last night, I went out late, and got another bag. But just a fifty this time, right. But I'm scared I won't be able to stop. I haven't slept since night befo last. My skins itchin. I feel like everybody know and they gon kick me out. What should I do?"

"Honestly, I would talk to Hugh. Tell him. Tell him everything like you just told me. And he'll help you out. He'll work with you. That's what he does. He won't kick you out. Not for being honest and going to him first. But if someone suspects you, and tells Hugh, and he comes to you first, tests you, and you fail, you'd be out. That's his job."

"You right. You right. That's why I came to you. No one else knows. I'm scared. But I'ma talk to Hugh tomorrow. But I can't get over the fact that I just threw thirteen months down the drain. Anyway, just don't tell nobody. I know you ain't. You seem real strong in your recovery. That's one of the reasons I came to you. Say, how long you got now?"

Matthew looked down at the desk calendar. It was October sixteenth.

"Seven months. Seven months today actually. I got here on three-sixteen, March sixteenth. Wow, it doesn't seem that long now looking back."

"Well, you doin good. Momma say you can come home, right?"

"Yep, sometime around Christmas."

"That's a gift right there. Well, thanks for talkin with me. I just needed to bounce that off someone right quick. I'ma talk to Hugh tomorrow. Say, good lookin out."

"Of course, man, anytime."

'Would I come clean in that situation?' Matthew thought.

Over the next six weeks, Matthew attended more meetings than he had since showing up at the Home. What he had seen from Ty scared him. He didn't want to end up like that. He even started to go to the old meeting where he had met Alex when he'd go to visit his mother on the weekends. But he still drank every Saturday night and started to on Friday's now as well. And he still found it unbelievably difficult to control his intake. However, he had a solution, go to more meetings.

He also tried to be as helpful as possible whenever he could. He helped new people to move their stuff in and rolled Willy outside whenever he wanted some fresh air. He even started volunteering, all to prevent what happened to Ty from happening to him. But refraining from partaking in his weekend escape was off the table. He needed that.

His relationship with his mother steadily improved, and the thought of soon leaving the Home occupied nearly all his thoughts. He wasn't present. His body may have been at the Home, but his mind was elsewhere, with his mother and the contents of their kitchen fridge. His soul was torn between the physical and the mental, balancing his increase in participation around the Home and the temporally diminishing fantasies of home. But it was his spirit that was the most noteworthy aspect of his being. It ached. It yearned for something greater, something higher, something magnificent but simultaneously craved the lower, something lesser, something base.

IX

I'm at the Men's Home. I stole some of mom's stuff and sold it to get high I broke her trust. If I killed someone I'd be in prison I'd have ruined someone else's and my own life and caused mom insufferable grief. I am at the Men's Home. Mom is at home alone. She's okay but she's healing I hurt her. I broke mom's heart when I stole her things her mother's things. It's funny how we can recover it's funny to think about the complete one-eighty we can do it's as funny as it is cringy to think about the way we used to live. Alex isn't trying to ridicule me he's trying to help he wants to see me succeed. Everyone's not out to get me only myself. I'm not crazy I'm sick I've been sick. I'll only go crazy if I don't get help continue to get help. Basically I was crazy. There's no grand plot against me other than the one I create that tells me to get fucked up. I did do something to mom I stole betrayed her trust. Mom wasn't sick of me she was sick of my behavior. I'm paranoid I'm thinking delusional thoughts. Alex didn't set me up. He has no reason to. I never have a good time because I manufacture my own misery when I'm drunk and high I don't have fun because my addiction produces pain. God doesn't hate me he loves me. God doesn't hate me he loves me. Mom doesn't hate me mom loves me she loves me so much she couldn't stand by and watch me slowly kill myself any longer and so forced me to get help. I made a mistake I'm cleaning it up now but I made a mistake. Just because I don't currently have the passion for God that Hugh has doesn't mean that I won't ever recover. Belief. Yes belief. Yes belief that alcohol and drugs will no longer rule my life. Belief that I'll go home. Belief that I can have a happy life. If I work I can buy cigarettes as well as other things. Dad's not mad at the me now he's mad at the old me. Forty-four is way too many people for a house. I don't have to fight anybody or anything if I just do what's right. I'm not qualified to work much of anywhere minimum wage but if I go to school I could get a better job. Dad'll probably reach out if I stay sober. If I believe that God can heal I can look another man in the face and divulge my secrets my past own it and be okay with it. God knows my past he knows everything about me. Of course God knows. If I start drinking and taking drugs again it'll undoubtedly be worse there's no doubt that I would hurt mom again it's inevitable. No there doesn't have to be a next time I can stop. I stole some of mom's stuff. There's no use going through life trying to fight everyone when people piss me off walk away it'll only get me in trouble. If I don't have rent money they'll kick me out it's the way of the world. Hugh would have to kick me out. Mom will only take me back if I get better. I don't drink like that I don't drink casually. I should go to a meeting. Whether or not he was trying to help he's trying to separate me from mom. He asked me to move away with him to take me from mom. I'm not sure why he said 'let him know' maybe he wasn't listening. There's a good chance he just wants me to humble myself again. Because he is my father and I'm his son simple as that. It's not a betrayal of mom to have a relationship with dad but that doesn't mean I have to I just can't use that as an excuse anymore. Feminine features aren't restricted to women. I have untreated alcoholism if it's not all treated it's untreated there is no half treatment. He knew I'd be on the line because he planned to show up late and have me take his shitty job. He was up to playing me buying himself time for his shitty job to be taken by me. Astroworld closed towards the end of 2005. He just knew how the job worked. A lot of white people are racist at least subconsciously a lot of times it comes out as condescension. There is a double standard that white people hold in regard to language. I stole quarters change it all starts and ends with change. I stole grandma's silver change. I would have taken anything whether it had value or not. She eventually got the quarters back. It happened in the closet. Coins but I didn't trade them to Leo. I was high. No one in their right mind would trade for chairs. I don't need any oxy. I don't want any oxy. My sister. Yes my sister. I quit my job at the linen service I put myself in a dangerous situation put myself around a crazy woman with access to drugs led to a relapse. If I got caught I'd be kicked out of the Home possibly arrested and prolong my suffering…no mom. If they thought I was fucked up they'd test me and then kicked out arrested suffering no mom. A handful would knock me out maybe even kill me with my lowered tolerance. If mom died I'd be absolutely devastated I don't think I could go on I'd die from the agony the grief. Yes people can die from a broken heart. I don't think I could live with myself if mom died because of me I'd kill myself. Then a lot of people wouldn't like police horses. No it's not BDSM. The Boston Marathon bombing. Then prison. Too far at the bottom of the sewer. If I'm tested I'll get kicked out. Urine a week saliva two to three days blood one day hair one month at least. That guy was drunk. He had no idea. He didn't know me. In the past I would've fucked him up. I was once a real asshole trying to fight everyone. I still think I'm tough. But I used to think I was real tough shit. The only way to make something of myself is to get sober. I got here through a broken family and years of drug and alcohol abuse. That's just how life goes I got here through a broken family and years of drug and alcohol abuse. I sold them I bought drugs I got high. Hugh wants to see if I want a job. Hugh didn't see anything. Lester didn't tell. Hugh's not going to test me at the moment. She could've had an STD. Hugh'd probably work with me if I didn't have rent money right away. I'm not going to be tested at least not right now. Then he wants to talk about something. He's not going to test me. Hugh didn't see me with that woman. I might get kicked out if he did. There's a good chance. He probably wouldn't care personally but his job would make him. Lester didn't tell stop worrying. Mom would be very disappointed. Then I'd probably have it too if she had something. An STD. Through tests or symptoms. Then Jerry gave it to her then she gave it to me or she gave it to both me and Jerry. If it was me that had something first then she now has it tasted it. I don't know if the length of time for contact makes a difference. I was high on power not sexuality I was in control that's why. She could've had a pimp. That's a hundred sixty small cups and eighty-one large ones if I were to split it about down the middle providing forty dollars to the small and forty and a half to the large and of course eight chips and eight candy bars at a quarter a piece. We're technically not allowed to it's illegal to resell donated food. Because he steals money from the drawer to buy lottery tickets. That wasn't his actual profit he sold more than that. I need to start eating right and exercise maybe even get on insulin. It means if I would've started taking better care of myself when the doctor first told me that I was prediabetic it could've gone away but I was too busy drinking. No with diabetes there's supposedly a period where you're borderline before you go full-blown. It's not reversible now. Yes it's too late. Not if I get healthy now. Stay sober. There's lots of places. Spiritual religious and health and fitness places perhaps to meet a woman. God knows you better than you know yourself you can't outthink him he wants to help when you struggle if you'd let him allow him to lead you. Because George knows it applies to almost everyone. It's both personal and communal spiritual advice. So he can take money out the envelope. Because when people are around he'll take the money later on his way to deposit it when he's alone but when no one's around he just pockets it right there. So he can take money out and then total it later. He didn't touch my change. You can't move on from something and still act on it it's one or the other you can't do both. Ty relapsed. He wanted to know what he should do if he should come clean. No I wouldn't come clean if I were in his shoes I haven't come clean about any of the relapses I've had so far so what makes me think I'd do it now.'

X

The day had come for Matthew to leave. It was December twenty-first, and he went to say his goodbyes. He first crossed Fannin to knock on the door of the yellow house. A man named Daryl answered.

"Is Jason here?"

"Yeah, I think, hold on."

A few minutes later, Jason stepped out.

"Is it bout that time, patna?"

"Yeah, my mom'll be here in about an hour. Just wanted to say 'see ya' before I'm off."

"Yeah, man, we gon miss you round here. Just remember to keep it real and focus on God. You do that and you'll always be taken care of."

"Of course, man. I can't forget."

"And don't be a stranger. When you get yoself a whip, come through and holla at a playa."

"I will man, as soon as I get a job."

"Bet, I'll see you then."

"Alright, Jason, take care."

"You too, later."

Matthew crossed back over Fannin and knocked at the door of the gray house. George answered.

"Hey, old boy, you off?"

"I will be here soon. I just wanted to say goodbye. I'm gonna miss you."

"I'm gonna miss you too, old boy. But it ain't like goin away forever, you're gonna come visit, ain't ya?"

"Absolutely, as soon as I get a car."

George chuckled. "Well, that might take a lil longer than expected. I been workin on getting one for a couple years now. But you can take public transit, can't ya?"

"Yep," said Matthew smiling.

"And I got your number."

"Yep," he repeated.

"Then this really isn't a goodbye cuz we'll be in touch."

"Yeah, I guess you're right about that."

George opened his almost toothless mouth wide and gave a hearty laugh.

"Don't lose sight of what's important, God, sobriety, and family. Without the first two you can't have the third."

"I won't forget."

"I don't suspect you will. You got yo head on straight. Keep it like that."

"I will. I will. And remember George, I'll be by from time to time."

"I'ma hold ya to that now, old boy."

"Alright, George, have a good one."

"You too."

Matthew headed over to the office to see Hugh. He walked in to see him smoking at his desk.

"You outta here?" he rasped.

"Yep, I will be here soon."

"Well, I just want to say that it's been an honor and a pleasure to have been able to watch you grow over the past how ever long it's been."

"Nine months."

"Nine months, has it really been? You know, I got to see

something beautiful happen with you, that I don't often get to see. I've seen a spark light up in you, you got a healthy glow to you now. I've been able to see that light come back into your eyes. God is good. It's a shame, I don't get to see such miraculous transformations as yours more often. I remember when they first drug yo smelly ass in here. I shoulda taken a picture. You remember that night we first talked?"

"Of course, how could I forget? There was something about you I liked but I couldn't quite put my finger on."

"Me too. Me too. I've been able to see the power of God work on you. You know, I prayed for you that night, prayed fo you and yo mother. And look now, y'all gonna give life another try, that's beautiful, truly beautiful."

"Mm-hmm."

"Well, you be good now and be sure to come by every now and then. These motherfuckers round here could use a positive influence, a success story."

"I will Hugh. Thank you for everything. I'll see you later."

"Take care now," he rasped.

Lastly, Matthew went to his room to get his stuff and see Willy.

"Aright, Willy, I'ma miss you. I'm gettin ready to leave."

"Oh, man. You is?"

"Yeah, my mom'll be here soon. Do you need anything before I go, cigarettes, a hot dog?"

"Just gimme a hug."

Matthew leaned in to hug Willy, his shirtless body was smooth as they embraced. When they let go, Willy's eyes were watery.

"What's wrong, Willy?"

"Nothin, just gonna miss you is all. Where am I supposed to find someone else like you to help me out with things?"

"Well, I'm sure Hugh and Chef Davy and Ty won't mind doin a little more for you."

"I know, but it won't be the same. Anyway, you be good now and do what yo motha say."

"I will. I'll be back by now and then to see you."

"You will?" his eyes lit up.

"Yes, I will. We'll see each other again. Bye Willy," and he grabbed his backpack, and headed out to call his mother.

Outside, in front of the meeting hall, Matthew called his mother to see where she was at.

"Hello," she said kindly.

"Hey, mom, I was just wondering what time you'd be here."

"Don't worry, I'm gonna get you. It'll be about twenty minutes."

Matthew felt funny. 'I'm gonna get you.'

"Okay, see you soon," he said and hung up perplexed.

'I'm gonna get you.'

A crash of glass woke him up. His mother stood before him in double. "Get up!" She threw another drinking glass at the wall right above his head which exploded in a shattering smash that rained broken fragments down around him. "I said get up!" she snarled. Trying to sit up, the beer that was perfectly balanced in his lap spilt over, pouring down his crotch and because he was laying back on his shirt as well. He couldn't feel the warm liquid enough to care and slumped further back again. His mother returned with a broom and smacked him hard once on the crown of his head. He stood up dizzy, swaying, with little control over his motor functions.

"What are you tripping about?"

"What am I tripping about? What am I tripping about! You god damn motherfucker you. You fucking drunkard. You junkie. I didn't believe it when your sister told me. I couldn't believe it. You sold my mother's stuff for this?" She held up a tiny baggy with five blue pills in it. "And this?" she motioned with her hand three small lines of blue powder on her coffee table.

"No, I didn't. She's lying."

"I already checked; you piece of shit."

She lunged at him and grabbed his shirt. He slid through it, shedding it in a remarkably nimble movement. She stood holding just his shirt. "You son of a bitch. I can't stand you like this anymore. I've had enough." She moved at him, and he ran staying just out of her reach. They moved like two magnets' like poles, with her repelling him further away. For a minute, she chased him ineffectually around the living room. She then picked up the broom again and smacked him in the face with it. He slowly stumbled back clumsily and fell. Moving up to him, she grabbed his wrist, but he yanked it free. He then drunkenly crawled a few feet until he had enough momentum to get up. He looked at the front door, and then back at her. "Don't do it. I'm gonna get you." He darted towards the door, she trailed him, but he managed to throw it closed behind him to momentarily buy himself a few precious feet. He ran sloppily out into the street and stood to catch his breath. "I'm gonna get you," she yelled from the porch. A car swerved around the corner at a high speed and just barely missed him. He looked towards the woods on the other side of the street, and then at his mother. She was quickly coming at him. He dashed into the thicket, running through thorns that slashed his legs and bare torso while sliding through mud. He could still hear his mother yelling when he got into the denser woods. He walked exhausted and drowsy until he made it to the two-lane highway on the other side. He continued physically depleted and mentally vacant along the road with his thumb out. About an hour later, he saw his home group's building in the distance. Upon nearing it, the familiar sight caused him to collapse, knowing he was finally safe, into the ditch parallel to the road.

He sat on the meeting hall step lost in the remembrance. He couldn't get it out of his mind. It was all coming together now. But why now? Now that he wanted to forget. Now that he had moved on. Now that things were starting to resemble what they had long before. About twenty minutes later, his mother's car pulled up.

As he stepped into his mother's car, both anxious and eager for a fresh start, he held in mind his newfound knowledge of being chased away. In coming, she drew him near, and yet she too was apprehensive about his return. They sat in momentary silence, both breathing in the body and mind, mind and soul, soul and spirit, spirit and essence of the other. Each clung to a shaky optimism for the home life ahead, whether out of folly or love or both, neither knew. The car pulled forth first gently and soon accelerated to great speeds. As Matthew looked out of the tinted window to the cityscape, and then redirected his gaze to the face of his mother which poured over with love, he of all people knew the least of what his journey in life would hold for him or even if the ability for him to recover was feasible. United once again, they made their way from one home to another with a delicate uncertainty in mind.

Acknowledgements

This project would not have been possible without the help of many friends and family. Foremost, I would like to thank my mother. Making amends will be a lifelong project. I would also like to thank the following people for not giving up on me, as well as showing me true friendship: Kathleen Park, John Walkington, John Shiflet, Leah Singer, Mike Ray, Mark Slade, Charlie Parfet, Kevin York, Jesse Jensen, Lalo Gallegos, and Walo Martinez. Such a list, however, will always be incomplete. Lastly, I would like to thank Joy Mazahreh. Without her emotional support, I might not have seen this project through to completion. For your love and kindness, I am eternally grateful.

About the Author

Michael Williamson was born and raised in Houston, Texas. He attended the Universities of Houston and Vermont. He currently attends Binghamton University in New York. He spends much of his time reading and outdoors.